If you are reading this book and did not purchase it or win it from an author sponsored giveaway, this book has been pirated. Please delete it from your device, and support the author by purchasing a legal copy from one of its many distributors.

No part of this book may be used or reproduced in any form or by any means electronic or mechanical, including photocopying, recording, or by any information storage and retrieval systems, without prior written permission of the author except where permitted by law.

Across the Street
Published by Sandra Marie
https://sandramarieauthor.wixsite.com/sweetsandra/
Cover Design: Makeready Designs
Editing: CookieLynn Publishing Services
Formatting: CookieLynn Publishing Services

The characters and events portrayed in this book are fictitious. Any similarity to real persons, living or dead is coincidental and not intended by the author.

Copyright © 2018 Sandra Marie
All rights reserved.

romance for all seasons #2

SANDRA MARIE

One

Steven lowered his phone, gripping it with an iron fist as he slumped on the front porch couch. Well, there went his whole reason why he was back in Seattle. The one that got away was gone for good, and being the gentleman his grandpa always told him to be, he took Cassidy's message and said being friends was a-okay with him.

It was a bold-faced lie.

He bent forward, tightening his laces and making sure his shoes were up for the miles he was about to put on them. He needed a new pair, but it was still a few days before payday.

It wasn't exactly running weather, but Washington was sticking to its signature rain. Steven tugged on his hood, stood and shook out his legs, and took off down the sidewalk.

In, out, in, out... The mind-numbing would start soon, he knew it. His eyes caught a glimpse of one of the neighbors across the street, and he politely waved when she looked up from her book. Her brows twitched slightly, and the smallest of smiles crossed her lips before she returned to her story. Steven focused once again on his breathing, taking the next turn off his street and past college row.

His grandpa had lived in the same house since he

bought it in the fifties. Over the course of Steven's life, he had witnessed oldies move out and young college kids move in the neighborhood. He'd wondered often if his parents had survived that crash if he'd be in Washington at all. From what his grandparents had told him, Mom had her sights on Alaska.

But if he'd lived there, he never would've met Cassidy. His gut lurched, his phone a dead weight in his pocket. Guess it didn't matter anyway—he'd lost her, and she wasn't ever coming back.

He shook his head and picked up the pace. *In, out, in, out...* He was supposed to be numb by now, but Cassidy's face popped into his head with each breath. She still wore those adorable glasses. Her hair was longer than it was when they'd dated, but was as naturally brown as it always had been. Cassidy wasn't the type to dye her hair. She was more concerned over the next Marvel movie theory and too career focused to wonder what she'd look like as a blonde.

The last time he'd seen her, she had that angry flush in her cheeks that he longed to cure. Her parents—her divorced parents—had been fooling around in her bed, and she was a little more than peeved. He couldn't blame her, even though a selfish part of him was thrilled that she called him to rescue her. He'd gone home that night walking on air, ready to make up for breaking up with her years ago.

He scoffed. What a pipe dream that turned out to be.

He slammed into a puddle, and water spattered up his legs. Sprinkles of rain soaked into his hood and mixed with the sweat collecting on his forehead. He looked up at the next street sign. Three miles. He was in the run three miles, and he was still pining.

He turned his feet around and sprinted back home, frustration rolling down his spine. Grandpa most likely was ready for bed, and Steven's sister, Jemma, probably wanted help with the laundry.

The numbness came to his fingertips first, the cold crawling up his arms and finally to his brain a mile away from home. He grinned, soaking in the methodical beats of running. Right foot, left foot, *in, out*, crack in sidewalk, again… again… heartbeat fast, faster, *in, out*…

He turned onto his street, and his neighbor looked up from her spot on the covered porch, her book perched neatly in her lap, a worn, oversized hoodie covering her torso and draped over light brown hair, the ends tinted blue. Her back straightened, and an awkward, yet determined smile appeared on her lips. She lifted a hand, her fingers trembling as she waved.

Steven half-grinned, taking in an easy breath. "Must be a good read," he said, keeping his pace, but turning around to run backward across the street. She jerked a little at his voice, and she mumbled something unintelligible.

"Didn't quite catch that," he said with a laugh, stopping in the middle of the road. The rain picked up, and if she wanted any chance to be heard, she was going to have to shout. But by the way she curled into her faded blue hoodie, he doubted she was even capable of anything louder than a whisper.

Her jaw clicked, and she took a large gulp. She held the

book near her face and gave it a thumbs up. A chuckle rose from Steven's gut.

"Maybe I'll borrow it sometime," he called out through the rain. "Have a good night."

She nodded, and in the light of the street lamp, her cheeks blossomed crimson rose.

Gorgeous, he thought, then turned to his own porch. Jemma sat on the couch his grandpa had put outside when Steven was fifteen, pressing her lips together in amusement as he shook his hair out.

"Showing off for the girl across the street, I see."

"Was not."

She snorted, her breath blowing the dark bangs off her forehead. "Oh yeah… all guys go running in the rain past cute girls all the time." She deepened her voice. "I'm Steven. Look how muscular I am. Look at my pecs showing through my white shirt. Look how not out of breath I am."

He wrinkled his nose and rang out the water from his hoodie t-shirt. Okay, maybe he was a bit nipply, but it wasn't on purpose. No wonder that girl was as red as a tomato.

"What are you doing outside?" He bent down and wiped water on her leg. She punched him and scooted away.

"Grandpa's doing yoga in his underwear again. I love the man, but he needs to wear pants."

The screen door banged open, and two excited Labrador pups tripped over their giant feet and mauled him.

"Hey, guys, I know… I know… I'll take you next time," Steven said, rubbing the ears of his six-month-old labs. The chocolate one leapt in between him and Jemma and nibbled on his ear. The white one, who was a little on the small side, still hadn't quite mastered the jumping thing.

He would've taken them on his run, but it was a lot of scolding and less running, and Steven had really needed to clear his head—even if it did take five miles for that to happen.

"I'm Steven," Jemma imitated. "I've got two adorable puppies and six-pack abs."

Steven shook his head. "No one's even out there."

Jemma sat forward and pointed straight across the street. "That girl hasn't left the porch since you told her to have a good night."

Steven's gaze followed his sister's finger, and through the thick rain he could make out her figure. She was in her seat, knees curled up and book nestled on top of them. Bright pink socks covered her feet.

"You want to tell her you're in love with someone else, or should I?" Jemma teased, but it dug deep in his chest, twisting and gutting him. "Don't want to get her hopes up, right?"

Steven moved the chocolate lab from his lap and stood up. "Hey, will you keep an eye on them?" he said, trying to keep his voice level. "Batman likes to run off."

Jemma tucked her hands under Robin, who was still bouncing around her feet, and cuddled with the pups. "Don't take long. I'm not nearly as fast of a runner as you."

Steven headed inside to shower. Grandpa was indeed sprawled out in the living room, donning only boxer shorts, stretching into downward facing dog. His pot-belly hung heavy over the waistband, and white hair sprouted like wild grass on his chest.

"Don't take too long, son," he said, his voice gruff. "I'm gonna need some hot water."

"No problem, Grandpa." Steven shut himself inside the bathroom and squeezed out of his wet clothes. His shorts hit the tile with a *thlump*, and he bent, digging his phone from the pocket.

His run was a bust; the second his phone was back in his hand, his fingers were already scrolling to Cassidy's last message. His heart sunk into the pit of his stomach, pounding thick and heavy.

You're coming to Thanksgiving dinner this year, right? I have someone I want you to meet.

It was accompanied by a shining picture of her, his beautiful best friend, her smile bright and excited, her eyes lit unlike he'd ever seen. And next to her, looking just as happy, was a man he'd never met before, but by the way the guy kissed her cheek, he was someone Steven never wanted to.

two

Ginny licked her lips and fluffed the pillow in her lap, eyeing the wine tray on the coffee table. She'd never tasted alcohol, even though she had turned twenty-one two Augusts ago. What if she was a lousy drunk? Or a crazy drunk? Or a mean drunk? There was something too nerve-wracking about losing control over her mind and body or tongue.

"You know what I loved?" her best friend, roommate, and book club founder, Lauren, said, bringing Ginny's attention up to the book discussion.

"There were five copies available in the library?" Jemma quipped. The book club girls laughed, and with the cue that it was okay to laugh, Ginny softly chuckled behind her book. Lauren playfully stuck her tongue out at the newest member and shook her head.

"Well, yes, that was a bonus. But I really loved Olivia."

"Totally!" Ashlynn said so enthusiastically that her wine sloshed about in the glass. "Olivia kicked ass."

The girls laughed, but Ginny only nodded in response. Truth was, the main character in the book was hard for her to relate to. Every decision she'd made went against all of Ginny's natural instincts.

"What'd you think, Ginny?" Lauren asked, and Ginny's heart beat triple time as ten eyes turned on her. This book club was way too crowded. This *house* was way too crowded. All but Jemma lived in one of the rooms, and it was the sole reason she could afford to stay there. When Lauren had invited her in the clubhouse—the nickname all the residents called the place—she'd said yes before really thinking about how many new people would be around.

A fist locked around her throat, and she gulped, trying hard to find her voice. She liked the book, but it was hard for her to say out loud. Her roommates were just going to lob more questions at her. Why she liked it, what her favorite part was, what she thought of Olivia... on and on until Ginny panicked over whether or not she was giving the right answers... even though she knew there were no wrong answers in an opinion. She just didn't want to offend anyone.

"It was good," she squeaked out, clutching the throw pillow in her lap tighter against her chest. *Book club is good for you*, she reminded herself for the umpteenth time. *It helps you socialize*. But oh how she wished it was good weather for biking right about then. She'd be out the door and on the thing in a second, letting the breeze and the road take away her anxieties.

Lauren leaned forward, soft encouragement in her light brown eyes. Lauren knew a thing or two about social awkwardness, but being older and in her element—books, books, and books—she was more on her game. Ginny took comfort in the fact that she wasn't the only one who shrank in the crowd. Lauren wasn't an outgoing person, but she could still encourage Ginny to peep out from her hiding spot from time to time. Ginny hoped to one day return the favor.

She cleared her throat, and her gaze darted to the pillow lining as she ran her fingernail across the stitching. "Olivia was so… out there," she said. "So confident. I felt a little… I dunno… envious of that, I guess."

She kept her eyes cast downward, letting her opinion settle in the book club without her overanalyzing everyone's reactions.

"Okay, Ginny, I have no idea how you aren't confident." Jemma flung an arm out, waving it up and down Ginny's frame. "I mean, just look at you."

The girls laughed and drank, and Ginny locked eyes with the neighbor. It was Jemma's first book club with them, and she'd teased Lauren, drank her fair share of wine, and kicked her bare feet up on the coffee table. Her shoulders were down and relaxed, her black hair tied in a messy side braid. She was the only one not living under the same roof, yet she spoke like she believed in her voice, which was more than Ginny could say.

"Um…" she stuttered, not sure how to respond. "Being… I dunno… pretty doesn't always translate to confidence. Not that I think I'm pretty or anything—"

"Why not? You should this that." Jemma finished off her glass and gestured for a refill. "My brother was gawking at you just the other day."

Heat ran through Ginny's neck and face, lighting the room up brighter than the wine. Her gaze darted to Lauren, her eyes screaming for some help. Lauren was right on cue.

"I think what set Olivia apart was her confidence in her

voice. She really believed in herself, and not just because she had the perfect body."

"What is the perfect body anyway?" Ashlynn said, flinging her arms out. Ginny's stomach leapt slightly as the wine got awfully close to splashing on the carpet. "Every body is perfect in someone's eyes, but never to the person who actually owns it."

"And that's the confidence I want," Jemma added. "In mind, body, soul… All that deep stuff I'm too drunk to talk about right now."

Ginny's shoulders relaxed, and she smiled her gratitude at Lauren for swinging the subject off of her. She sat back and listened to the girls get increasingly more vocal about things as the wine lowered in each glass. A calm settled over her as her voice stayed behind bars, only coming up every so often to make a comment here and there when prompted, but Lauren was the queen of diverting the other girls' attentions.

As the sun started to set outside their big living room window, Ginny's thoughts drifted to going back to work in the morning, doing the same thing over and over until she clocked out. The mailroom at Mills Advertising wasn't glamorous, but it was quiet and didn't require her to talk to a lot of people. In fact, silence was encouraged. Her coworker didn't really get that memo, though. Alex was loud and proud and everything Ginny wasn't. It was a miracle they could stand each other.

There was another position opening up, though, and Ginny had looked up the requirements as soon as she'd heard about it. She'd taken the year off to save up and start her master's program, and moving up in the advertising business would build her confidence to help her do what she really wanted. Therapist was her ultimate goal, but how could she help anyone when she couldn't even voice her opinion in book club?

The corners of her mouth turned down, and her shoulders slumped. There was no way she would get that position upstairs, let alone her master's degree. They all required the one thing she didn't see herself ever having—courage.

She eyed a psychology book on the side table next to Marcy, one of the girls who lived in the basement. Was there a point to pursuing that dream?

The doorbell cut through her thoughts, and Ashlynn jumped. It was a good thing her glass was finally empty or it would've gone all over.

Lauren and Jemma laughed, and then April, the other basement room owner, peered out the window.

"Oh… it's that hottie tottie brother of yours, Jemma."

"Leave him out there to rot!" Jemma joked, calling loudly enough Ginny was sure Jemma's brother heard it. The girls drunk-laughed, and Ginny turned to the door, hoping someone would get up and open it while she darted to the bathroom until he was gone.

Jemma leaned forward and pushed on Ginny's knee. "Hey… you should answer it."

"What?" Ginny choked out.

"You want to be confident, right? Be brave. Put

yourself out there."

"I guess… I just didn't mean…"

"Then answer the door. It's just Steven. Seriously, he's like a bunny rabbit. He's all meat and muscle but fluffy and way too nice for his own good."

Ginny looked to Lauren, her saving grace, but her best friend tilted her head, almost like she considered the suggestion a good one.

Ashlynn was no help either. She was singing under her breath and staring at her hand like it was the most fascinating thing on her body. And Marcy and April leaned forward and joined in the peer pressure.

Ginny pleaded with Jemma with her eyes. *Please don't make me do this.* But it was no use. Jemma sighed dramatically and fell back into the couch. "Guess he's going to stay out there forever."

Ginny's palms slipped from the pillow she clutched, her blood rushing in her ears as she turned around in her chair and eyed the door. It was nothing. She'd answered plenty of doors in her lifetime, and since she was determined to be on her own someday, she should answer every time that chime went through the clubhouse. Her legs cracked as she unfolded them from the chair, her muscles stiff from sitting so long. She nibbled on the inside of her cheek, wringing her hands together each step closer to the door.

It was fine. She'd spoken to him yesterday… kinda. It'd taken the entire run of his for her to be brave enough to smile and wave. It was partly because of how handsome he was, with his black, cropped hair and Superman build, and partly because Ginny took forever to talk to anyone new. She'd seen Steven running, biking, walking his two adorable puppies. She'd seen him helping his grandpa unload groceries, reading on the porch, teasing his sister. He seemed a genuinely nice person, which made it all the more nerve-wracking to put her hand on the doorknob and twist.

The door creaked open, and she was met with smile lines and gorgeous ocean blue eyes. A plaid button-down hung open, revealing a graphic tee that clung to his muscular torso. Skinny jeans hugged his lower half, and two labs, one brown, one white, bounced playfully at his feet, their leashes tangling together. It simply wasn't fair how attractive he was.

"Hey," he said, and Ginny wished she could find her voice to say it back or be witty and smart like in the movies. She simply smiled—or tried to—and waited for him to continue.

"Hate to bug you about this," he said, holding out a measuring cup, "but I'm out of milk, and the mac and cheese is at the point of no return."

An unexpected giggle rumbled up her throat. Ginny covered her mouth, shocked that such an easy thing as laughing happened without her trying to stop it.

"Um… sure. We do milk. I mean have milk." She closed her eyes and shook her head. "Come on in."

"Are they okay to…?" he asked, pulling on the leashes. The pups lurched forward, trying to climb up Ginny's legs, but Steven had a tight hold on them.

"Sure, but keep them away from the wine."

He chuckled, stepping inside. Jemma popped up from

her chair, toasting him with her empty wine glass. "Did you just bring the puppies to show off?" she teased. She tipped her glass back, then frowned when there wasn't any more wine.

"Should've kept the wine from my sister," he said to Ginny, almost like they were sharing a secret. Were they joking together? Her heart thrummed with excitement, and she used it to bolster her voice out of hiding.

"I'll, um… grab that milk. How much do you need?"

"A third cup should do it."

She held her hand out for the measuring glass, and for the briefest of moments, their skin grazed one another. Her breath caught in her throat, and she shot back, flames licking her cheeks. She bolted into the kitchen, glass in hand, internally cursing herself for freaking out over such minimal contact.

The girls' voices floated in from the living room, occasionally interrupted with the deep voice of the attractive guy and the playful barks of his puppies. She wondered how it was so easy for everyone to talk and laugh and socialize, and she wished for the hundredth time that day that she was in that category.

Her eyes fell to the measuring cup, and she snapped the jug back, sloshing it around. Whoops, she'd gone a bit overboard, and the two cup measuring glass was almost full. She laughed at herself and tried to put it back, but it was a giant mess, spilling over her hand and wrist and onto the counter. There was another half gallon in the fridge, so she decided he could just have the rest of the open gallon.

After pouring what she could back into the jug, she twisted the top on, washed the measuring glass, and took a deep breath. There was no time for nerves; he had mac and cheese on the stove.

She put on a smile and tried to casually stroll back into the living room. The puppies were having a field day with the girls, crawling on them and licking faces. Books had fallen to the floor, and wine glasses were forgotten. Steven held his hands up as his eyes locked with hers. "This was all them, I swear."

Did she come across as uptight? She hoped not. It was the cutest scene she'd ever stumbled into.

"Um... here," she said, handing over the jug. "We have another in the fridge, so you can... if you want, it's fine to take the rest."

"Thanks a lot," he said, his voice genuine and friendly. She was careful not to touch him as she passed it over. "Let me know when I can repay you."

"Don't... yeah, don't worry about it."

"You sure?"

She nodded, jumping a little when the chocolate lab hopped over to her. She reached for his soft ears. The little guy calmed down so much he slumped to the floor and cuddled against her feet.

"Wow," Steven said. "Teach me how to do that?"

"Hey, dork, she just showed you," Jemma teased. "If you want to ask her out, find a better pick up line."

Ginny's heart shorted out. Steven lifted a brow, but was otherwise unfazed by his sister's lack of filter. He turned a friendly smile to Ginny's steam-filled face and held up the milk jug.

"Thanks again." He then addressed everyone. "See you around, ladies."

He gathered his pups and left. Ginny's breath didn't return till the door clicked shut.

"You did it," Lauren said as Ginny curled back into her chair and grabbed her trusty pillow. "Was it as bad as you thought?"

Ginny would have to think about it. On the one hand, she'd said more than two words, so that was progress. On the other, she didn't think she'd return to a normal color anytime soon.

three

"C'mon, I know you're hungry," Steven said, holding out the mini bottle to the tuxedo kitten. The cat was being a stubborn little shit, refusing to eat or drink anything that wasn't from Mom. Unfortunately, the mom cat had disappeared, and the litter had been brought to the shelter earlier that morning.

Steven sat on the tiled floor in the kitten room, five tuxedo kittens prancing around his crossed legs, begging for more from the bottle while their brother turned his head away, his mewling cries echoing around them.

He sighed and set the bottle down, scratching the top of the kitten's head. "I get it, dude. It's rough being left behind. But you can't ignore your stomach forever."

He settled the kitten in his lap and picked up another, her eager mouth wrapping around the bottle immediately, spraying her face and Steven's fingers.

"I relate very much to that kitten," a familiar voice came from the doorway. Steven steeled himself, plastering on a fake smile that he turned on his best friend and love of his life. Cassidy crossed the room, her Wonder Woman jacket dangling off her purse as she plopped them both into a chair and took a spot on the floor across from him. She plucked up a kitten and wriggled her nose against its fur.

"If I was a pet person, I'd take him."

The corner of his mouth perked up. "She's a her, actually."

"I'll call her Scarlett."

"For Scarlett Witch or Scarlett Johansson?"

She shook her head, her glasses slowly sliding down her nose. "You know me too well."

"DC is better," he argued, nodding toward her Wonder Woman jacket. She sighed, like they'd been over this a million times—which they had, but it was part of their rapport—and picked up another kitten.

"You never answered my text," she said frankly, running her long, slender fingers down the soft black and white fur. "Still debating on if you want to witness the drama?"

She was teasing, but hurt ran through her tone, piercing his heart. He bit into his tongue, an apology sitting there that he didn't mean. But if it made her feel better, he'd do it. That's what labeled him as a good friend, a nice guy… the one who finishes last.

He took in a deep breath and stroked the stubborn eater in his lap. "Does that mean your dad will be there?"

Her bottom lip jutted out in that way he used to tease her about. There were days when he'd kiss that look away, sweep her up in his arms, and they'd spend the rest of the night kissing, sleeping, happy… Now he had to sit and watch that look, unable to do a damn thing about it.

"He's still a maybe. Which is why I need you. I need a buffer."

"Isn't that what your boyfriend is for?" he bit out without thinking. He quickly laughed it off, hoping she missed the bitter tone.

"I meant a buffer between him and them," she said. "Can you imagine my mom blabbing about how all men are awful creatures and then sneaking a quickie with good ol' Dad in the closet? Um… no. I need friends there. Grandpa, and Jemma, you…"

Silence crept in the room, all except for the mewls from the tiny kittens. Steven mindlessly fed them, battling his brain and his heart. He wished he could tell her no, that he wasn't ready to be in the same room with her and her boyfriend when all he wanted was to be the one holding her hand, joking around with her, having the same arguments and inside jokes they always had.

He wanted to tell her the truth but it would hurt her, so he kept it locked inside. She was most likely oblivious to his feelings. He'd broken things off in the first place. The fact she was sitting across from him like they hadn't been in love at all was a white hot dagger to his chest. Had he meant so little? Did he still?

Who was this guy who'd stolen her heart, anyway? He bet the guy had nothing on him in the nerdy knowledge department. Probably couldn't run a 5K backward or do a triathlon in less than three hours. Did he make her laugh like Steven had? Could he get any girl he wanted? Because Cassidy was not just any girl.

"Can I bring someone?" he blurted, heat blurring his thoughts and making him stupid.

Cassidy perked up, her smile wide and beautiful, her gapped teeth just as adorable as always. "Heck yeah! Is it serious?"

"Getting there, I think." Lies. All lies. They spewed like a geyser, and Steven couldn't grasp them and cram them back in. "We planned Thanksgiving together."

"That's great!" And damn it, she actually looked happy for him. "Please bring her." Cassidy pushed off the floor and wiped her butt free of cat fur. "And let me know if you guys want to bring a dessert or rolls or whatever."

"You bet. She's a great baker. She'll probably want to." Shit, what was he doing?

"Can't wait to meet her." She grabbed her things. "I want a picture."

He nodded. "Uh... my phone's in my locker."

"No rush. I actually gotta run, but I'm so happy you're coming." She bent down and wrapped an arm around his shoulders, and for a moment he forgot the BS he'd just spewed and concentrated on how warm she felt, how she smelled of vanilla and sugar cookies, and how much he missed holding her.

He watched her go, frowning behind her before he quietly yelled at himself. "What the hell?"

How was he supposed to find the perfect date—who could bake, no less—in three weeks? He was so hung up on Cassidy that he'd barely taken notice of anyone else. He grasped the back of his head and cursed under his breath. He was just so willing to one-up her, wanting to prove he hadn't moved back home just for Cassidy. Maybe he wouldn't come off so damn pathetic. Now he was screwed.

He tried feeding that stubborn kitten for the rest of his shift before passing him off to the on-call vet. The other kittens would be ready for adoption in another week or two. If the little guy wanted to join them, he'd better get his head out of his ass.

Maybe Steven and that little guy had a lot in common today.

He slid on his jacket and scrolled through his phone, hoping for a name to pop up in his contacts that he could get to spend Thanksgiving with him. Nope, nope, nope… Did he know anyone who was still single besides his sister's friends?

He stepped onto the sidewalk and made his way to the grocery store a few blocks down. Speaking of his sister's friends, he owed them some milk. His gorgeous neighbor had said not to worry about it, but Steven wasn't the type of guy to not pay back a favor. He paid for two gallons and started the cloudy journey home, his thoughts a jumbled mess.

four

Must be personable, willing to talk up the business to potential clients. Knowledgeable, fast learner, and confident.

Ginny frowned, grabbing the lid to her laptop and easing it down. She had three weeks to find the courage to apply, and that was just the first step. Imagine the interview. She'd bet her entire paycheck management would spend one minute with her and write her off as too shy to be in advertising.

She tapped her nail against the laptop and sighed, gazing across the street. Grandpa Atkinson was in the front yard, raking the leaves in nothing but an undershirt and sweatpants. Ginny shivered, pulling her crocheted blanket around her shoulders. It was getting chilly, but not enough to stop her from sitting on the porch. She liked the crisp smell of autumn and rain. Washington had been good for the craving.

Maybe Grandpa Atkinson needed help. That was something she could try—put herself out there and actually talk to the neighbors. It was worth a shot.

She pushed from the padded chair, fingers curling around the blanket while she talked her courage up. Awkward silences were her nemesis, and the worst part was she had no idea how to fill them. She hoped Grandpa

Atkinson was a talker. If he was anything like his granddaughter, Jemma, she had no need to worry.

The blanket slid from her shoulders, and she plopped it into her vacant chair. She hugged her torso and hopped down the three steps to get to the sidewalk. Their street wasn't busy, but it didn't stop her from stalling, checking three times for cars before crossing the road.

A soft hum greeted her as she stepped a foot onto the crunchy grass. Grandpa Atkinson twirled the rake around, his tune awfully Christmas-themed for November.

Ginny tucked a strand of her turquoise-tinted hair behind her ear, nerves shaking her core. She could turn around before he noticed her. She didn't even have a rake or a garbage bag or anything but her two trembling hands.

Her eyes slammed shut, and she shook her head, turning back toward the clubhouse.

"Hey there." Grandpa's gruff, yet friendly voice stopped her. She slowly swiveled to him, trying a smile. He leaned against his rake, a patch of gray underarm hair making heat rush to Ginny's cheeks and her eyes to find the cloudy sky much more interesting. "What can I do for you?"

"Um…" she told the sky, her fingers, the ground… "I didn't know if you… I thought maybe you might want some help?"

He shifted, and she chanced a glance up. He had the same grin as Steven, and she imagined he looked much the same when he was younger. He had the kind eyes of a handsome soul, and the hands of a man who'd carried his family through life.

"Help?" He gripped the rake. "No. But I'll never say no to some company."

The air thickened, and Ginny tugged on the sleeves of her sweater. She preferred helping over sitting and watching the old man work, but when he gestured to a camp chair sitting near the front porch steps, she couldn't walk away. That would've been just as embarrassing. And rude.

She eased into the seat, shivering at the fresh mix of cold and nerves that hit her.

"So," Grandpa Atkinson said, resuming his work, "you're friends with Jemma?"

Her voice was a tiny squeak. "She's in our book club."

Grandpa Atkinson tapped his ear. "Gonna have to speak up for this old fool."

Great. "Um…" Ginny sat straighter, hoping that helped her project. "She's in our book club."

"That's right." He dragged the rake across the lawn, stuffing the leaves into the growing pile. "I about hit the floor when I saw her with a book."

A small smile twitched at the corner of her mouth. "Is she… not much of a reader?"

"Jemma?" His head fell back and a joyous laugh left his lips. "If it weren't for the subtitles on the TV I gotta use for this hearing of mine, I'd think she'd forgotten how."

Ginny pursed her lips, holding in her amusement. She wasn't an avid reader, not like Lauren who was constantly with a book, but she enjoyed sinking into a world that wasn't her own. She had a great respect for self-help non-fiction authors, and looked up to authors of text books. The written word was the reason she'd gotten this far in life in the first place. She couldn't imagine a life when it didn't play such a defining role.

Yet Jemma seemed so content, happy, like she knew who she was already. At twenty-one.

"So what's your name, sweetheart?" Grandpa Atkinson continued, dragging the rake through the grass. Leaves crunched and crackled under the pressure.

"Ginny," she said softly, then cleared her throat and repeated it louder.

He grinned that handsome grin and rested the rake against the porch railing. "Well, Ginny, feel like helping me out with these leaves now?"

She hoisted to her feet and scanned the grass for a bag but couldn't find anything.

"Did you want me to bring the garbage can around?" She jut her thumb over her shoulder. Grandpa shook his head and laughed, gesturing her forward. He reached for her hand, and Ginny's heart pounded in her throat.

"I wasn't raking to throw them away," he said, bending his knees and eyeing the pile with childish wonder and mischief. Ginny caught on seconds before the old man jumped, dragging her with him with a loud crackle.

A surprised yelp escaped her, and she spit out a leaf that flew onto her tongue. Grandpa Atkinson laughed and flapped his arms, grabbing handfuls and chucking them toward Ginny.

She sat stunned for a moment, nervous for about twenty more seconds, then shakily grabbed her own handful and tossed it toward him. Laughter shook her stomach, heat in her cheeks from joy and not embarrassment for once. She lay back, spreading her arms wide and joining Grandpa Atkinson in making leaf angels.

When they found the grass, Ginny leapt to her feet and raked the leaves back into a pile around Grandpa Atkinson, burying him up to the neck. He made a lot of talking head puns, all of which had Ginny laughing and cringing equally. A rush of excitement ran through her, and she took a brave plunge, leaping into the pile next to him.

"I haven't leaf jumped since I was probably five," she said through a smile, hoping her voice carried over the crunching and crinkling.

Grandpa Atkinson's eyes widened. "One should never stop jumping in leaves. Or finger painting. Or running through the house in their underpants."

"I'm pretty sure I've never done that," she said, suddenly understanding Jemma's "Grandpa's underwear" jokes the other night. She fell back, using the leaves as a bed and staring up at the sky. How would it be if she could live like the Atkinson family for a day? They were all so outgoing, uninhibited.

The leaves shifted next to her as Grandpa Atkinson rested on his back. His arm came into view, and he pointed out the clouds. "What do you see?"

She tilted her head, forming the cloud into something in her mind. "A marshmallow...?"

He snorted. "All those screens kill creativity in young brains."

Heat flared through her cheeks, but she bit back laughter. "What do you see?"

"Firetruck." He traced it with his finger. "Alligator." A long sigh floated over them, and Ginny rose on her elbows, heart pounding when she locked eyes with ocean blue irises. Grandpa Atkinson groaned and sat up, pointing at Steven. "Now I see judgment."

Ginny pressed her lips together, scrambling to her feet and sweeping her body free from the leaves. Grandpa stayed planted in the pile.

"Don't let me ruin your fun," Steven said, eyes drifting across Ginny's body. She plucked more leaves from her sweater and let them float toward Grandpa Atkinson.

"Too late." Grandpa Atkinson lifted his hand, and Steven helped him to his feet. "You finally get us some milk?"

Ginny followed the old man's gaze to a pair of gallons on either side of Steven's feet. Did he carry those home from the grocery store? Ginny could barely get it from her bike basket to the kitchen without her fingers going numb.

"One is ours," he said, bending for the jugs. His eyes swung to meet hers, and chickening out, Ginny looked at the leaves instead. "The other is for her."

"Son, if you want to court a lady, you buy her flowers."

Steven shook his head, giving Ginny a look like they were sharing some sort of inside joke.

Grandpa Atkinson grabbed one of the milks from Steven and then nodded them off. "Well, walk her home at least." He patted Ginny's shoulder, swiping his thumb gently across her jawline. "Had fun with you, Ginny. Make sure to do that more often."

"I... I will."

He grinned and hummed his way inside. Steven turned a raised brow at her.

"We were... I was helping him rake," she stuttered, tucking her hair behind her ear.

"He pulled you in, didn't he?"

"Maybe."

Steven silently chuckled, swinging the gallon over his shoulder as they started across the street. "That old man."

"He's fun. I like him," she defended. Enjoying life like that was so rare, especially for her. She lived most of her days in a constant state of fear, but for a moment, she was just a girl playing in leaves, and it felt wonderful.

"Me too," Steven said, love for his grandpa resonating in his eyes. A static buzz ran through her chest, and she dropped her gaze, fighting the attraction. Steven was far too handsome and charismatic and nice to ever bat anything but a friendly eye toward her.

That was okay. Better, actually. Thinking of Steven as a friend might make it easier to interact with him.

She climbed her porch steps ahead of him, turning at her door. "Um..." she began, pulling on her sleeves. "Thanks for the milk. You didn't have to..."

"I wanted to. You saved our dinner last night."

He held the jug out to her, and she took it, their hands brushing. Her breath stuttered, and her heart triple-beat, but she didn't run. Progress.

She hugged the gallon to her chest, the cold causing a ripple of goosebumps up and down her arms. He stepped forward, and she instinctively backed into the door.

"Sorry," he said. "You just have…" He reached out, plucking a leaf from a chunk of her turquoise tips. He smiled and wished her a good evening, and she stood there, the ghost of his touch resting in her hair.

Must be confident, she thought as she eyed her laptop on the chair on the porch. She took in a deep breath and took a shot.

"Um, Steven?"

He swiveled on the bottom step, tilting his head.

"I… I was going to make some cookies. Do you… I mean, if you have nothing else to do…"

His smile widened, cratering his cheeks and lighting his features. "Sure. But I'm not much of a cook."

Neither was she, if she was honest, but it wasn't so much the baking that she wanted help with. She opened the front door, standing back from him to go in first.

"That's okay. I… could actually just use the company."

 five

The clubhouse smelled like a library, and Steven chuckled to himself as he stepped into the small living room, scanning the many paperbacks piled on the side table. The only books in his house were the ones on his e-reader app.

"Um... Kitchen is through there," Ginny said from behind him, her voice just barely over a whisper. He wasn't sure if she was trying to keep it down for her roommates or if she was naturally timid. He thought the latter, but he didn't know her well enough to assume anything.

He crossed the living room into the kitchen, the faux wooden floor a lot like his own across the street. A small table was flush against the far wall, and more books littered across the leaf designed tablecloth. The smell of pumpkin spice rose from a dwindling candle resting on top of the fridge.

Ginny moved to the cupboard, pans slapping together as she dug for a cookie sheet.

"Festive," he pointed out, leaning against the counter and picking up a glittery pumpkin. He tossed it in the air and caught it. "You don't usually see Thanksgiving stuff. People like to skip right to Christmas."

She grabbed the fridge handle. "Lauren wanted to make things look... autumnish, I guess." She lifted a shoulder and fished out butter and eggs. Dark Sharpie indicated both items were hers. "Could you, uh…" She pointed to the cupboard behind him. "The sugar is in there."

He swiveled, the cupboard door creaking as he opened it to three packs of sugar. He picked the middle one, tilting his head in amusement over how she wrote her Gs. It wasn't capitalized, but larger than the rest of the letters.

"Brown sugar, too?" he asked, spotting it on the lower shelf. She nodded, and he added that to the growing pile of ingredients. "Sweet," he said, picking up the peanut butter. "You're doing peanut butter?"

"Chocolate chip peanut butter cookies." She nibbled on her bottom lip. "Thought I'd give them a try."

He set the jar down. "You bake often?"

Her honey-colored eyes widened, and she slowly shook her head. "Not… not really, no. I just… Well, I wanted to say thanks to your grandpa, and cookies are neighborly, right?"

"You want to thank him for tossing you into a pile of leaves?" The corner of his mouth twitched. "He'll love 'em… if he can get to them before Jemma."

She seemed relieved, but a nervous energy rested over her. The world seemed a bit too large for her.

"That's awesome," he said, gesturing to a dark outline of a bike on her wrist. "You just get that done?"

Her eyes drifted down. "I… Kinda. I drew it."

"You're kidding." He wrapped his fingers around her sleeve and pulled her hand close to get a good look. The ink looked professional, the lines on the bicycle so detailed.

"What'd you use? A marker?"

She didn't answer right away, and he lifted his gaze to her slightly open mouth and her unblinking eyes. One by one, he unwrapped his fingers from her sleeve, and her breathing slowly returned. He hadn't scared her, had he? It wasn't his intention, that was for damn sure.

She blinked and fumbled for the spatula on the counter. "Momentary ink," she said softly. "They come in bottles that you can mix. It'll stay on for a week or two."

"Hmm," he said. "Maybe I should give that a shot. I'm too indecisive for the real thing."

She cracked an egg into the bowl. "I know what I'd do. It's the needle part that scares me."

"Oh, I'm not thrilled about that either."

Her shoulders relaxed, and a gorgeous smile lit in her eyes. An electric shock ran through his chest, and he shifted slightly.

"I…" she started, then shook her head and mumbled a soft, "never mind."

"What?" he encouraged. She was cute, and every word she spoke seemed to take so much effort. Maybe that was what made everything she said sound so important.

She poured the sugars and mixed them with the peanut butter already in the bowl. Her breathing went in, out, in, out… much like his on a run.

"I… was just going to say… that, well, maybe I'll get the courage to do it for real soon. Before Thanksgiving."

"That is soon." Didn't he know it. He had twenty-one days to find a serious girlfriend and parade her about in front of Cassidy just to save face. He picked up the sugars now that Ginny was done with them and put them back on their shelves. "What's so significant about Thanksgiving?"

She lifted a shoulder, the blue ends of her hair softly brushing against the bare skin of her collarbone where her sweater had fallen loose. "I like schedules, I guess."

He raised a brow. "Someone you're hoping to see on Thanksgiving?" he prodded jokingly. "Impress them with your newfound courage?"

She let out a hollow laugh. "I wish that were the reason. But there will only be me to impress this holiday season."

"You're not going home for Thanksgiving?"

"My parents are in Italy." She slid over and started rolling the dough into big, sticky blobs and slapping them on the cookie sheet. Steven washed his hands and helped her out.

"And roommates? They all got plans?"

She nodded. "It's… it's okay. I don't mind… being alone."

The soft way she spoke made Steven think that was one hundred percent true. She probably preferred being alone; perhaps that was where her comfort lived. But a light flickered on in the back of his mind, growing brighter as it formed in his head.

It was an insanely selfish thing to ask, and he opened his mouth three times and slammed it shut to debate some more. The thing was, he wanted to be selfish. He rarely was. And he didn't want to admit to Cassidy he'd fabricated a girlfriend just to make her jealous—which seemed to backfire badly, anyhow. The mess he'd made earlier spun panic in his chest, and as Ginny settled the cookie sheet into the oven, he let his panic take over his tongue.

"Okay... I've got kind of a problem, and before I get into it, I just want to double check... You really don't have any plans for Thanksgiving?"

Her brows pinched, curiosity painting her face. She shook her head.

"All right." He took a deep breath. "Here goes. I want to be full out honest with you, here, so you know what you're stepping into. If you agree, anyway."

She let out a small squeak of laughter. "You're starting to sound like... Well, like me."

He stepped forward and leaned against the counter next to her. "So... my ex and I have done Thanksgiving dinner every year we could. Our families switch off hosting, and it's just a tradition now."

"That's not awkward?"

He held a finger up, tapping his nose. "Sure as hell is. What's Thanksgiving without a little awkwardness?"

She smiled, her gaze drifting to her wrist. She pulled at her sleeves, covering the temporary tattoo. The image of her doing that at Thanksgiving and taking her hand in his solidified his decision to at least ask.

"Thing is," he continued, "this year, Cassidy—my ex— she's got a boyfriend. And well, I'm still very much *not* over her."

Ginny jerked back, and a flicker of pain or shock swept through her irises and was gone in a blink. The corners of her lips turned down, and she let out in a small voice, "I'm sorry."

He wanted to tell her it was okay, but it wasn't. He hated how Cassidy had moved on, how he'd lied to her, how he was willing to keep on lying just so his ego didn't come off so bruised.

He let out a long breath and stared at his shoes. He really did need new ones. "When she asked me if I was coming this year, I spewed out that I had a girlfriend."

"And... you don't?"

He shook his head, a hollow laugh rumbling his lips. "Pathetic, right?"

She didn't answer, and after the longest silence, he tipped his head back. "Geez, you could at least tell me I'm not pathetic," he teased.

A small chuckle escaped her. "I don't think you are. I... I get it, I think. It's hard to feel... left behind."

"Yeah." That wasn't exactly it. He felt just a step too late. "Anyway, I know this is crazy, and I don't really know you, you don't really know me, but... Would you join me at Thanksgiving?"

"As your girlfriend?" she squeaked, her elbow knocking into the oven door. He quickly waved his hands.

"No, no... I mean, yes, but not for real."

Her brows scrunched, and his heart sunk. Had he just made it worse? Had he just let another potential friendship crash and burn?

"Pretend I'm your girlfriend..." she clarified. He frowned, shame creeping through his bloodstream and painting him red.

"I know it's a real jerk thing for me to ask."

"A little…" she admitted, gazing at the floor. She traced the lines in the wood panels with her boot, her teeth pulling at her bottom lip.

Steven ran a hand over his face. He was unbelievable. How could he have asked flat out like that? That wasn't who he was. He was the sit back and take it kind of guy. Think of others first, himself second. Suck it up and be miserable. Nice guys finish last, after all.

"Hey, forget it," he said, pushing off the counter. "I was being stupid, and I'm so sorry."

Her honey eyes lifted, meeting his without an ounce of animosity. Surprising. She should've kicked him on his can already.

"When do you need to know?" she asked.

"Huh?"

The smallest of smiles lifted her lips. "I'd like to think about it. Is that okay?"

He straightened. Was she serious? "You sure?" he checked. "I mean, it's not the best thing of me to ask."

She rubbed her hands together nervously, staring at her shoes again. "You… Well, you seem like a nice guy. I don't think you would've asked unless…"

"Unless…?"

She shook her head. "I don't know. Unless you were… really hurt or something."

So she'd noticed his beta male personality, too, even though he'd been a level ten jerk a few minutes ago by asking. His nice guy label must be tattooed on his forehead.

"You're right," he said. "But it isn't your problem. I'm sorry for asking you."

"I'd still like to think about it." Her eyes finally met his, determination resonating in the tightness of her jaw. "Give me a deadline?"

Oh hell, he didn't know. "Before Thanksgiving," he joked.

"Well, yes… but how soon before Thanksgiving?" She toed the floor again. "I mean, we'll have to learn a lot about each other, right? Be convincing?"

"I guess… yeah." Was this really going to happen? The idea of walking into Cassidy's mom's place with Ginny on his arm put a confident smile to his face. Ginny was gorgeous, there really was no other word for her, but she was also sweet as pie, and he'd owe her if she did this for him.

"Okay." She straightened her back, her stance much surer than her voice. "I'll let you know by the end of the week."

He nodded, still in shock over his luck that she'd even consider it. "Okay."

They both let out awkward laughs, and a distinct burning smell wafted through the air. His nose wrinkled at the same time as hers. She dropped her mouth in the cutest oh-no expression.

"The timer!" she gasped, spinning around and opening the oven to a pile of smoke. Her mouth was set into a frown as she pulled the black cookies from the oven and plopped them on the stove.

"No offense," he said, "but I'm not sure Grandpa will eat those ones."

six

Ginny slid the mail into the slot and tucked it into the cart for the fifth floor. The mailroom was empty, except for her, that morning. No surprise there. Alex, her coworker, was never on time, especially lately. She assumed it was another girl who'd caught his eye. They never stayed long, but when they were around, Alex never was.

She sighed and moved onto the next batch. It'd been a long morning, and not just because it was the beginning of the month, which was always busiest. But her mind kept rewinding and replaying Steven's face when he'd asked her to fake a relationship with him. She'd only been trying to have a conversation with the guy, which had been hard enough. Pretending to be a girlfriend when she'd never owned that title would be a completely different ballgame—one she wasn't sure she'd ever be ready for. She couldn't disappoint him, though. The guy seemed heartbroken enough.

"Hey, uh... mail girl." Caleb from the online department popped his head inside. Ginny pulled her headphones down, letting them rest around her neck.

"You got a few minutes to do a coffee run?"

She jerked back and pointed a lousy finger at herself. "Um... me?"

He let out an impatient sigh and held out a credit card. "Intern called in sick, and the bosses are dying without caffeine. Head to the cafe two blocks south of here. Ask for Mill's Ad's order, got it?"

She nodded, ripping her headphones off and stuffing them into the drawer with her purse. She could do a coffee run. There wasn't even a need to order. In and out, and then she could get a peek of life outside of the basement.

She rolled her bike down to the cafe, grateful for the basket attachment, even if it didn't look awesome. As soon as she had the cups, she took every bump with extra care. Luckily the cafe was only three blocks, and Ginny was a pro at cycling.

As she propped her bike against the rack, she spotted Alex just walking in for work. His hair was a bed-ridden mess, the same hoodie he wore the day before hanging low over his jeans. He had a bag from the burger joint he visited at least once a week, which he used to wave at Ginny before bumping his back against the door to open it.

"See ya on the inside, Gin Rummy!" he called out, his mood tangible in the mid-morning air. Ginny's cheeks flushed as a couple of girls giggled at either her nickname or her handsome coworker. It was a toss-up. Alex got a lot of attention for his outgoing personality and the fact that he looked like he should be on the company's ad roster and not working in the mailroom. But no matter how friendly or handsome the man was, he was a big pain in her butt. By the time he sauntered in for work, Ginny had already sorted through most of the mail—the worst part of her job. Yet, he was the guy all the upstairs people knew.

She picked up the coffee holder and headed inside. *Must be confident*, she thought, the words on from the job opening running through her head. If she had any hope of returning to school, she needed to get a higher paying position.

Her heart beat unevenly with every step toward the elevator. It was going to be okay. If she could play in the leaves with the old man next door, she could certainly deliver coffee to the tenth floorers.

Her thumb shook against the button as she pressed it in. The elevator dinged and shut her in, and she took the few seconds she had to calm her breathing. *Just don't trip*, she repeated in her head. She looked down at her worn, reliable boots. They surely wouldn't let her down, not when she was finally upstairs.

The elevator opened, and the smell of freshly cleaned carpet and mints from the front desk floated in the air. The clickity clack of fingers on keyboards echoed around her, along with the occasional chatter from either phone calls or just office gossip. Ginny stepped forward, nerves wracking her body and stiffening her hand around the cup tray. She tried her best friendly smile and grabbed the attention of the receptionist.

"Hi. I have coffees for the meeting in—"

"Yep, just down the hall to your left. Stop back here for your tip. I just have to get approval."

"Oh, I um… no… I actually work here."

Confusion filled the receptionist's eyes, and she gave

Ginny a once-over. "Where, exactly?"

"The... the mail room."

The receptionist nodded like that explained her. Was what she wore so out of place? Ginny analyzed her outfit again, wondering if it was the tights or the shorts or the oversized button up over her tank top. It seemed appropriate she supposed for the mail room, when the only other person to see her most days was Alex. But the receptionist wore a loose blouse over a skirt, heels on her feet. Warmth rushed through Ginny's face, and she tugged at her clothes and made her way to the conference room.

The dig at her attire did nothing to help build her confidence. Would she stick out like a sore thumb in there? Or would they just be happy to see their drinks? She paused in the hallway, shaking her hair out. Odd hair color wasn't frowned upon in this particular office, but her nerves had her doubting every single detail about herself.

And it was only coffee.

She spun on her heel and nearly bumped into someone barreling toward the conference room.

"Um... excuse me?" she asked. Blood rushed through her ears as the man turned around. "Could you... Are you headed to the meeting?"

He blinked, almost as if his train of thought had been derailed. His eyes drifted to the coffee. "Oh! You have the coffees, excellent. I can take them in."

"Thank you," she said, equally relieved and disappointed as she handed them over. She made a speedy exit, pressing the elevator button multiple times to get her downstairs. As soon as the door shut, she fell against the back wall. "Must be confident," she whispered to herself. "Must be completely... not like me."

She twisted her hair around her hand and pulled, debating on chopping off the ends when she found a pair of scissors. Her hair was the only adventurous thing about her. It'd taken three weeks of going back and forth on the decision and finally taking the plunge the night before Halloween. The blue wasn't even that noticeable in her brown hair, unless she was in the right light, but it was still more daring than anything else she'd done.

The doors opened up to the mailroom, and she grabbed her headphones. The sooner she blocked out the thoughts running through her head, the better.

Alex was rocking out near the piles of mail she'd already sorted, grabbing the packages and setting them on the wheeled cart. He was at least there to take care of those. The thought of hand delivering the mail had Ginny's hands shaking.

"The big guys celebrate when you saved the day with caffeine?" he teased, shoving a roll of junk mail into the recycling pile. Her eyes fell to the ninja teddy bear tattoo on his toned and tanned forearm. He'd played it off as a drunken decision, but she wondered if it had more meaning to him. She couldn't imagine any tattoos holding no meaning whatsoever.

She rubbed her wrist, the momentary ink of the bicycle showing the first signs of fading. If she ever got over her fear of... everything... she'd put the drawing she kept hidden in a jewelry box on her hip.

"I could go all day without the stuff," Alex continued, and it took Ginny a second to realize he was talking about coffee. She bit her lips together, holding in a snort. Of course he could; he got his full eight hours every night, if not more.

He snapped a rubber band around another roll of junk and tossed it smoothly over his shoulder. He whistled an unfamiliar tune, dancing around the room more than usual. Ginny never initiated conversation, but if she did, she would ask if he had good news or something. Alex was never too thrilled to be at work, preferring partying over sorting, and Ginny wasn't the most exciting of company.

"So, Gin Rummy," he said, popping her on the hip with a thick envelope. She jolted, eyes wide. He managed to hold back his laughter at her jumpiness. "You going out for the desk job?"

She blinked, her hands stilling on the pile for Ashton Mills, the CEO. "Are... I mean, do you want it?"

"Not what I asked." He spun a rubber band around his wrist, his brow lifting somewhat. The scar above his eye prevented it from fully rising. "But I don't know... You know what time they have to be here?"

"Yes," she said, straightening her pile. "It's the same time we're supposed to."

He gasped, grappling at his chest like she'd shot him. "Touché, Gin. Are you finally getting a backbone?"

A wave of heat washed over her, and she hid her face with a curtain of hair. Alex either didn't notice or was used to her silence. He picked his whistling back up and chatted away like she hadn't just shut him out.

"It sure pays a pretty penny, though. Gotta say, Ashton almost has me convinced to shoot for it."

Her gaze darted over. "He... the CEO talked to you about it?"

He nodded, his head bopping to whatever music was running through his one earbud. "Said I'd have a good shot if I applied. Guess it's my magnetic personality."

Her lip lifted in the corner, humoring his joke, but disappointment crawled through her chest and drowned her heart. With Alex going for the job, she'd have no chance. He could put as much effort in as he did for everything—minimal—and still win out over her. It didn't matter that she was always on time, that she had her bachelor's degree, that she knew more about the business. She lacked that one defining factor of a good assistant accountant rep—confidence.

She was really starting to hate the word.

She slammed the pile of mail down and let out a fake cough. "Can you take care of this?" she asked. "I'm not feeling well."

"You're going home?" An incredulous look crossed his face. "*You?*"

She coughed into her fist and reached for her purse. "I'll be in tomorrow."

"O-kay," he said, waving her off. "In the future, you don't have to lie about it. Just leave like I do."

And you'll still get the job over me. She blew out a sigh and shrugged into her jacket. Her fingers fumbled over her bike lock, frustration blurring her vision. She was not going to let some slacker take the higher paying job, especially if he didn't want it.

An idea cropped into her head, taking shape in the midst of her anger. Determination and urgency propelled her speed, and she hopped on her bike and pedaled toward home. She'd better get to the Atkinson's before she changed her mind.

seven

Steven unhooked the latch on Cocoa's leash and set the wriggling pup loose in the exercise area of the shelter. The fluffy brown Pomeranian mix had been given up by her owners earlier that week, and was just now willing to let him take her outside. She carefully treaded the grass on her little legs, her ears flapping in the November wind. Poor girl was so shy, and Steven would bet she was still waiting for her previous family to come back for her. But they were most likely in their new house by now, settling in without their pup.

He bent and stroked the top of her head. "It's all right, girl," he said. "You got the whole place to yourself right now. Better enjoy it."

She shivered in the crisp cold air and tentatively sniffed the ground. All he needed was for her to go to the bathroom, but he wished she would run, play… It killed him every time a sweet dog was dropped off on their doorstep. One day he'd get his own place and foster them all until good families rescued them. It was his dream, in fact. The shelter was just a stepping stone.

He pulled his phone out and snapped a few pictures. She was sweet and good photos did wonders for the adoption website. The one up of her now was taken just a day after she was dropped off, her ears back and her tail between her legs. She looked like a scared baby bear cub and not the little three-year-old dog that she was. Maybe if he got some good shots of her interacting with humans she wouldn't come off so timid. If only she'd stay still for a selfie.

He crouched to the grass, crossing his legs and picking her up under her fluffy belly. Her ears fell back while he snuggled her. Damn it, he couldn't get attached, but if he could take away some of that heartbreak, he was going to darn well try.

"How about we look at some pictures, huh?" he said, settling her in his lap and pulling his phone in front. She curled up like a cat, resting her head on his thigh. Her jitters ran up and down his shin. "You're a beauty in this one," he said, trying to show it off to the pup, but she wasn't having any of it. She huffed out a whimpered sigh and turned into his hip. He stroked her fur, trying to calm that shaking.

His thumb mindlessly flicked through his gallery photos, most of them animals at the shelter. His labs, Batman and Robin, were the only pair of that litter who weren't adopted, so he'd taken them both, promising himself—and Grandpa, who wasn't too thrilled—that he wouldn't adopt any more. But Miss Cocoa was sure tempting him.

"Who could leave you, huh?" he mused, flicking through more pictures. His heart sunk, and he paused, thumb hovering over a photo of him and Cassidy just last year.

He'd come home for the holidays, and they'd spent a night in a super hero themed escape room. Cassidy's bright face was in a state of shocked bliss, her fingers holding their record time on a printed out certificate. Their faces were so close together, smiles matching, and Steven remembered wishing they'd been in the room longer, if only to spend more time with her alone. Maybe apologize for ever letting her go.

He'd wanted to kiss her that night, but the opportunity never really arose. Guilt had held him back, and fear over how she'd react tied and bound him. He was lucky she wanted any kind of relationship with him, even a platonic one.

Warm breath washed over his forearm, and a soft snore escaped the now dozing pup in his lap. Sharp tingles pricked his left foot as the first signs of it falling asleep hit.

He sat for a while, letting his leg and Cocoa sleep. The air turned a bit colder as the sun ducked behind a large gray cloud. If he felt any rain, he'd nudge her awake and hopefully get her to go to the bathroom before cleaning out the rest of the kennels. He didn't mind dog duty, but he could go without scrubbing messes every day. Most of the dogs were trained, but none were made to live in a cage, and nerves and fear were just a recipe for accidents.

His phone vibrated against his knee, and he clicked out of his photos and answered. "Hey, she's taking a bit to go," he told Eric, his coworker who was working the front desk today. He figured Eric was bugging him to clean out the kennels now so they could jet out on time.

"There's someone here to see you," he said. "You want me to send her out?"

Steven's gaze drifted to the dog in his lap. Her trembling had stopped. "Yeah, that's fine."

It had to be Cassidy. He'd already agreed and lied his ass off about Thanksgiving. What did she want now?

He turned his eyes to the doors leading out to the exercise area, waiting to see her signature glasses, her long brown hair, her Wonder Woman jacket. Instead his heart jumped and brows lifted when a sweet pair of honey eyes met his; soft brown and turquoise hair blew in the wind as she opened the door, and she tugged on the sleeves of her oversized pink sweater, then hugged herself as she made her way across the grass.

"Um… hi," she said softly, stopping a few feet away. Steven grinned, unexpected relief and excitement that it was Ginny and not Cassidy relaxing his chest.

"Hey. Didn't expect to see you."

She lifted a shoulder. "Yeah, I asked Grandpa… I mean your grandpa… if it was okay if I stopped by your work."

"Hell yeah." He patted the grass next to him, and she nibbled on her lip, tucking a wind-blown strand of hair behind her ear before sitting. Her eyes turned to Cocoa, and he noticed a twitch in Ginny's fingers.

"She's real sweet," he said, stroking her fur. "You can pet her, if you want."

Ginny tentatively reached out, and the shake in her hands reminded him so much of the dog herself.

"She's so soft," Ginny said, a small smile crossing her

lips. "What's her name?"

"Cocoa."

She bent down and whispered into the fur at the top of Cocoa's head. "Hey, Cocoa Puff. You are just so sweet, aren't you?"

The dog sighed in content, nudging into Ginny's touch. Steven's attention shifted from the pup to the girl, her hair creating a cocoon around her and Cocoa, almost like they were both so comfortable in a smaller world.

"You're good with her," he said as the dog roused from her sleep and padded her way to Ginny's lap. Steven chuckled as strands of dark brown fur snagged into her tights. "You'll probably need a lint roller after this, though."

Cocoa propped up on two legs, resting her front paws on Ginny's chest and nuzzling into her cheek. The most adorable giggle left her lips, and she scratched the dog's ears. "I think… it's worth the shedding."

He reached across and tried to get in on the scratching, but Cocoa turned her butt to him, snuggling into Ginny's neck. He playfully scoffed.

"I think I just got snubbed."

"She knows you'll take her to that tiny kennel."

"You're probably right." He leaned back on his hands. "Feel like taking her home with you?"

A playful frown fell to her lips, reminding him slightly of Cassidy's pouts. Ginny was different, though. Like it wasn't normal for her to be so expressive. A tiny dimple appeared in her chin.

"I wish," she said. "Clubhouse rules includes no pets."

He snapped his fingers. "Darn. You two would've made a cute couple."

She tilted her head into Cocoa's fur, her light brown and turquoise hair mixing in with the dog's. He could picture Cocoa hanging around in her purse or in the basket of her bike or on a leash as she jogged. Maybe he could put some charm on and talk Ginny's landlord into letting her have a dog.

"So…" she started, still snuggling the dog, like she was trying to draw some courage from it. "I… Well, I'll do it."

He sat up. "What?"

"I'll be your girlfriend for Thanksgiving." She paused, taking a long, deep breath. "For a price."

His lips parted, but he wasn't sure what to say. He wasn't loaded, and he wasn't sure how much she would ask for. The whole thing was starting to sound a lot like a—

"But not like… I'm not going to be like, an escort or anything," she rushed out, her big honey eyes wide and panicked. Cocoa playfully barked and jumped against her chest, and the first smile Steven had ever seen on the pup wrapped around its little mouth.

He breathed out a laugh. "Okay… I was going to say I wasn't really comfortable with that."

Red splashed her cheeks, and she pinched her eyes shut. "I just meant… I need your help with something in return. If… if that's okay."

"Okay?" He lifted a leg, resting his elbow on his knee. "Of course it's okay. Anything you need, you got it." He couldn't believe she was actually agreeing to his nonsense.

She could ask him to bungee jump out of an airplane. He would rake the leaves in the clubhouse yard for a year. He'd bike her around to every errand or party or meeting she had. Whatever she wanted, she could have.

She twisted her hands in the dog's fur. Damn, he wished she could take Cocoa home. He'd never seen either of them so calm.

"There's... Well, there's this opening at my job. I really could use the promotion, but I'm not exactly... what they're looking for."

His forehead wrinkled. "Why not?"

She stayed quiet for a minute, squishing Cocoa's cheeks. Steven let her sit and gather her thoughts. She seemed to need the long pauses in conversation, and he was more than okay accommodating.

"I'm not exactly..." She bit her lips together and took another deep breath through her nose. Steven wanted so much to take her hands, maybe hold her through wherever her thoughts were taking her, but Cocoa seemed to be doing a good job of it so far.

"They want someone with a lot of charisma. Courage. Confidence. And I'm... Well, you've met me." A shy laugh escaped her, but it had no humor behind it. The smile faded quickly into a disappointed frown, her eyes cast to Cocoa as she continued to stroke the fuzzy pup. "I need the pay raise. I need... to learn how to be all those things." Her eyes lifted, meeting his with a flash of worry. "Like you."

Him? He wouldn't exactly call himself charismatic, courageous, or confident. He was in love with his ex, and his ex had no clue because he'd stood back and let her believe what she wanted.

"Will you teach me?" she said, her voice trembling. The wind blew a strand of turquoise-tinted hair across her face, latching onto her glossy lips. Her eyes grew more and more frightened the longer the question hung in the air.

Of all the things she wanted from him, it was something he wasn't sure he could deliver, but he would sure as hell try.

He clapped his hands together and pushed to his feet. "You'll get that promotion," he said, hoping to exude the confidence she was hoping to gain. She wriggled to her feet, a little awkwardly with the dog in her arms. Cocoa stayed put, something else she'd refused to do so far. He'd had to drag her around by the leash with her trying to wiggle free every time he tried to carry her.

"Good." She bit her lip and let out an awkward laugh. "So… when can we start?"

eight

Ginny swept a hand down her torso, brown dog fur flying from her sweater to the wooden floor in her bedroom. It was so hard to put Cocoa back into her kennel and say goodbye. She hoped the little dog found a good home soon. She deserved lots and lots of cuddles.

Her spirits bolstered after meeting with Steven, even if it was a little more than nerve-wracking stepping into this façade with him. But she could sense an improvement in her life coming soon, and hope that she'd creep out of her shell and take charge at work had her dancing around her room. She'd never do it in public, but in private, dancing for joy was totally okay.

She tied her hair back and flopped in the middle of her unmade bed, reaching across the mattress for a pad of paper and pen she kept in the top drawer of her nightstand. She worked so much better with a list or a plan of action, and she doodled across the top of the page with flowers and hearts around the words HOW TO BE A GIRLFRIEND.

Unfortunately, she had zero experience in that department, but she wasn't about to admit that to Steven. The dates she'd been on had been short with no sparks and mostly nerves. Ginny barely spoke two words, and she probably had bored all her suitors to death ten minutes in.

Talk more, she wrote as the number one thing on the list. That'd probably be good for her own agenda as well. She couldn't very well be in advertising without talking.

She tapped her pen against the pad, eyeing her phone sitting on top of her bed. She'd exchanged numbers with Steven at the shelter, and it had taken her three tries to get her number right as she'd typed it into his phone, her hands were shaking so much. He, of course, had no trouble giving her his number.

She set the pad aside, tiptoeing her fingers across the sheets and wrapping them around the cool phone case. Texting counted as talking, right? It was definitely less intimidating. She'd initiated conversation earlier, but it had taken her twenty minutes to get the courage to go inside and talk to him.

His number stared at her with no accompanying picture. It was a real shame she didn't have one of him; she could use a daily dose of dimples.

She tapped onto the message button and typed out a few openers before settling on one.

Are you doing anything tomorrow night?

That was bold—braver than a lot of things she was used to doing. She hit send and held her breath, falling into her pillows. This was insane. How did she fake date someone? Was it like really dating them, only without the feelings or kissing or holding hands? Because she was a pro at that already.

Too nervous to wait for his response, she pushed from the bed and stripped. She grabbed a towel and scurried to the bathroom down the hall.

She started the water and waited until the steam covered the mirror before hopping in. The hot water cascaded over her, rinsing away her thoughts. She had to stop overthinking things—stay focused on what she wanted. There was a reason she'd moved to Washington. There were reasons she wanted to keep going with school. More than anything, she wanted to help people like her, people who were afraid of themselves. Or, more accurately, people who were afraid to be themselves.

After letting the shower rinse away her nerves—and dog fur—she climbed out, taking a cleansing breath. She bumped into Lauren, her nose in a book while she talked to her boyfriend on the phone. She'd occasionally let out a "uh-huh" and "that's awesome, babe" before flipping the page. Ginny laughed to herself; she wasn't one to interrupt a good story or boyfriend time, so she silently padded back to her room.

A blinking green light shone from the top corner of her phone, and she held her towel together with one hand and picked the cell up with the other. As the screen turned on, her stomach leapt at Steven's name at the top of her notifications.

Walking the puppies. You wanna join me?

Then another message.

Let's do dinner, too. Wear good shoes.

She smiled, biting the inside of her lip and tapping the phone. She'd need to add more to her list, including agreeing to going out on dates.

Okay, she tapped back. *Five o'clock good with you?*

***

Ginny stood at the end of the clubhouse driveway, staring at the Atkinson's porch.

It wasn't a date. It was a fake date. Which was different... somehow. She didn't have to put on an act, for one. There was no worrying over if there would be a kiss goodnight or hand holding or if she'd be good enough for a second date.

She pulled at her running jacket, tugging the zipper up and down, up and down, up and down. The weather was good for a run, at least for now. The sun shined through a patch of clouds, and there was a slight breeze ruffling through the trees. A brown, crinkled leaf swung loose from the branches above her and floated to the gutter.

Her fingers curled, and she stuffed them into her pockets, taking a calming breath before stepping onto the road. Her running shoes fell heavy, pounding in tune with her heart as she crossed the street, made her way up the Atkinson's drive, and hopped up the two porch steps. She blew out another breath before tapping the screen door twice.

Cute little barks greeted her, and her fingers found her zipper again, toying with the metal while her teeth toyed with the inside of her lip.

"Guys, knock it off!" The door muffled Steven's firm but friendly voice. The pups didn't take him too seriously, barking still as he swung the door open.

"Hey," he said, holding the puppy collars with two

fingers. His black hair was wet, dripping down his forehead and soaking into his white graphic tee. He fumbled with the screen door, trying to open it for her and keep his dogs under control.

"Sorry, they're still in training," he said, holding the labs back as they tried to leap up on her. Ginny giggled, backing up as the very large paws of the white lab pressed against her hip.

"That's okay." She patted the dog's head, giving him the attention he was obviously lacking. "I… guess I found my walking buddy."

"If you want Robin, you take him. He's a distracted walker."

Steven grabbed their collars and coaxed them inside. "Have a seat for a second," he called over his shoulder. "I just gotta grab my shoes."

Her eyes fell to his socked feet, amusement curling her lip when she noticed a R and a L stitched into the black socks. Were his socks directional?

The scratching of paws on wood floor echoed through the space, and Ginny found a comfortable looking chair and sat gently on the edge, looking around the room. The house layout was a lot like the clubhouse, only they had carpet in the main living room and the Atkinson's was all wood, minus a red and black rug the couch rested on. A large TV hung on the wall, and a yoga mat was rolled up and resting against a standing lamp.

Where the clubhouse had leaves, pumpkins, scarecrows, and cornucopias, Grandpa Atkinson decorated his house with clocks and what looked like puzzles glued together and framed.

Ginny tilted her head to the side and squinted at a fox puzzle that had to have been at least twenty-five hundred pieces.

"It took him three months to do that one," Steven said from behind her. His breath was awfully close, washing over the back of her neck and sending chills down her spine. She was too nervous to turn around and meet his eyes, so she lifted her hand and ran her fingers over the furry animals in the puzzle.

"It would've taken me years," she said. "Or it would still be in the box."

He laughed, and it was only when she felt him put distance between them that she turned. Her eyes fell to his still shoeless feet. A pair of what used to be running shoes dangled from his hand.

"Um…" she asked, gesturing to the shreds in his hands. He lifted them up.

"Yeah… A couple of puppies are in big trouble."

She peered down the hallway, both of the puppies droopy, their ears back, and avoiding eye contact. She bit back a laugh.

"Feel like doing dinner here?" Steven asked, crossing into the kitchen and tossing his shoes in the trash. "We got the place to ourselves for a bit. Grandpa and Jemma are out on their date."

"Date?" she asked, following him into the bright kitchen. The walls were painted yellow, and the sun streamed in from the one window, reflecting off the white cupboards, making the whole room look orange.

Steven dug in a bottom cupboard and pulled a pot out. "Yep. Tradition in the Atkinson household. Grandparents take their grandkids on dates every Thursday night."

"And you aren't included in that?" She hoped she wasn't interrupting an important tradition for him just for the sake of a fake relationship. Steven shook his head, opening the fridge and clucking his tongue.

"No, actually. My dates stopped when Grandma passed. She was my plus one."

"Oh," she stuttered. "I'm… I'm sorry. I didn't…" Her words fell away and heat ran through her neck. She wrung her hands together and looked out the window.

A dimple appeared in his right cheek, and he shut the fridge and faced her head on. "Hey, it's all right. No need to get nervous over it."

Her eyes turned to giant circles, and she jerked back at his forwardness. "Um, okay."

He crossed the room, each step earning an extra heartbeat from her. "You want to learn confidence, right?"

"I… Well, yes." He was too close. She could smell his shampoo from his still wet hair. Did he shower before a run? Or was it just to get the pet shelter smell off?

"Speak like you mean it, then." He straightened his stance. "No more ums. No more wells. Just think about what you want to say and say it. Don't worry about offending me. Promise I can handle your opinion."

Something jittered in her chest. His blue eyes glinted,

and he leaned against the counter, waiting for her response.

Think about what she wanted to say? She'd completely forgotten what they'd been talking about.

"I… um…"

"No ums."

"Oh, right, um…"

"Whoops." He laughed, and a laugh of her own floated to her lips. She covered her face.

"This is hard. It's a natural part of my vocabulary."

"Is it?" he asked with a lifted brow. "Looks like you just went without."

She brought her hand down, her forehead wrinkling. How had he done that? Her heart was even beating slower, her breathing more manageable. All he'd done was make her laugh.

She watched him wander around the kitchen, opening and closing cupboards and peering in the fridge four times before she finally stopped him.

"You don't have any clue what to make, do you?" she asked, proud that she didn't say um once. She even added a hitched hip for good measure. Look at her go.

He turned a sheepish grin on her. "How do you feel about pizza?"

nine

The soft whine of his naughty puppies echoed down the hall, and Steven shushed Batman and Robin before putting the last bite of his first slice of pepperoni into his mouth.

"When did you get them?" Ginny asked, her voice soft. He had to pick up his listening game to hear her.

He reached for another slice and leaned his back against the couch. They'd plopped on the rug in front of the TV, but he'd kept the screen off on purpose. Getting her to talk a bit more would help her mission to break out of that shell.

"About a month ago when I moved back here." His eyes dropped to her nails as she plucked off the pepperonis and ate them separately from her pizza. "I was in Boston for school."

Surprise tinted her brown eyes. "Which one?"

"Don't get too excited," he joked. "Wasn't Harvard or MIT. I went to Northeastern." He paused, pumping his fist. "Go Huskies."

Amusement hit her lips around her small bites of pizza. "I was a Husky, too."

"Because dogs are the best."

She turned and eyed the back bedroom door where the labs were still crying. Her frown almost had him caving and letting them out, but they'd be all over the pizza, and they had to serve their time for the murder of his running shoes.

"What… I mean, are you going back to school?"

He shook his head and swallowed his bite. "I came back here to help out Grandpa and Jemma, get some experience in the shelter. But mainly I came back to—"

He cut off, his thoughts hitting his heart hard. Ginny tilted her head, a wrinkle appearing just above her nose. He'd already told her he wasn't over his ex, but he hadn't told her he'd moved back home solely to win Cassidy back. It seemed… rude to mention, almost. Or maybe more embarrassing than anything else.

She bent her knee, resting her chin on it as she ripped a piece of pizza off and slid it between her lips. She chewed carefully, slowly, patiently waiting for him to finish his sentence, but Steven wasn't sure if he would.

He shrugged, taking a sip from his water bottle. "What about you? How long you been living at the clubhouse?"

A loose piece of her light brown and turquoise hair fell from her ponytail, and she brushed it aside with her pinky.

"Just since September. It… I almost didn't get in."

"Is it like a sorority or something?"

"No, but the landlord only accepts people who are dedicated to rent for at least a year. I wasn't sure… you know, with my job if I'd be able to…" Her teeth came out and pulled at her bottom lip, her fingers twitching around her food. Steven cocked his head; what thoughts crept up in that brain of hers that kept her so quiet?

"You okay?" he prodded. Her eyes locked with his, surprise resonating in the browns of her irises.

"Um… yes. I guess. I just… Well, I was going to say…" She shook her head hard. "Never mind."

He scooted closer so his arm was a mere inch away from hers. There was a hitch in her breathing, but she stayed stone still.

"I was just… If Lauren moves, I'm not sure I'll stay."

"Why's that?"

"She's… She's covering part of my rent." She put her mutilated pizza down in the box and wiped her fingers off with a paper towel. "If I don't get a raise or this promotion… I'm not sure where I'll end up."

His chest tightened and twisted, and he gulped his pizza down, hoping to relieve the pressure. "You'll get it," he said. She seemed surprised by his confidence. "You done with this?" He reached for the pizza box, ready to shut the lid. She nodded, and he pushed to his feet. "I'm gonna let the demons out. Just a warning—if you stay on the floor, you're free game for pup kisses."

Her smile touched him deep in his gut, almost tilting him off axis. He'd spent some time with Ginny now, but he still wasn't used to the sudden blows when he realized again just how gorgeous she was. Her personality was just an addition to it, and he couldn't see why she'd want to change anything about herself. She was brave when she wanted to be, and that seemed enough for him.

He put the pizza in the fridge and took a sock slide down the hall to his bedroom door. "All right, all right, stop scratching the wood, guys!"

The moment the knob was turned, a brown and white

nose pushed their way into the hall, tiny paws slipping across the wood floor to get to the living room fast enough. Tongues dangled from the sides of their mouths, and an adorable squeal came from the living room when the pups found their target sitting on the floor.

Ginny tossed her head back and forth, dodging flapping tongues, screaming with delight as Batman hopped up onto the couch behind her and gave her a nice wet willy.

"I warned you," Steven said with a laugh. His heart was ten degrees warmer. He leaned his elbows on the back of the couch, pushing on Batman's butt to get him to sit.

"They're..." Ginny blew a raspberry after Robin licked inside her mouth. She stretched her neck, keeping the dogs away from kissing her. "They're just so happy."

"Too happy for being the bad puppies they are." He hopped over the couch and settled into the cushions behind her. He pulled on Batman's collar and scratched his ears to settle him down. Ginny squished Robin's face until he was so excited he had to find a toy for her. He came back with a mangled stuffed animal, proudly shoving it into her lap.

"Um..." she said, lifting it with two fingers. "What exactly...?"

"That would've been the Build-a-Bear I got when I was seven."

She pulled on what used to be a teddy bear face and lifted an eyebrow.

"Yeah... I should've kept him out of my stuff. Oh wait, I *did*." He playfully scolded Robin, who rested with his butt in the air, tail wagging wildly as he waited for Ginny to toss the mangled mess across the room.

"Can I... Am I okay to throw it?" she asked. Steven waved a hand out for her to go for it, and that gorgeous smile lit her face as she threw it high into the air, and Robin completely missed the catch. Steven hated to lose his shoes, but this was turning out to be more fun than the walk they'd planned.

"He's working on that," Steven said with a laugh as Robin pushed the bear back into Ginny's lap. Batman was perfectly content with the ear scratching... for now.

After a few more minutes of catch, Ginny's shoulders lifted with a deep breath, and she nibbled on her lip. "So... I um... Well, I think we should..." She paused, reaching into her jacket pocket. Her fingers nervously curled around a folded blue paper. "I have a list of questions." She started unfolding the paper. "Maybe I should... I don't know... Know these things about you before Thanksgiving."

He held his hand out for the list. "Let's see what we got, here." Amusement picked his lips up as he looked at the first one. "Pretty sure you already know my name, Ginny."

A splash of pink painted the apples of her cheeks, and she distracted herself with Robin. "But not... Well, I don't know your middle name. Or if you have a nickname. Or if you prefer to go by Steven. Or if I'm supposed to call you babe or sweetie or love pumpkin—"

"Please don't call me love pumpkin." They laughed together, and her shoulders relaxed. He adjusted on the couch, leaning his elbows on his knees, his leg grazing her arm. "What would you like to call me?"

"I'm… I'm good with Steven."

"Me too." He folded the paper. "And I don't have a middle name."

"No middle name?" She tossed the bear again, and Robin took his sweet time retrieving it. She must be tiring him out.

"Nope. Just Steven Atkinson. And no one calls me Steve. At least no one close to me."

Her eyes pinched in concentration, like she was filing away that tidbit of information. He grinned at her dedication.

"Okay," he said, sliding from the couch and onto the floor next to her. "Your turn."

"Um… What?"

"Middle name? Nickname? You want to be love pumpkin?"

She pressed her lips together, her eyes sparkling with withheld laughter. "Ginny Ann Thompkins. Most people call me Ginny, except for Alex who calls me Gin Rummy."

"Gin Rummy?" He grinned, pushing back his curiosity over who Alex was. "I like that." He wished he'd thought of it.

She crinkled her nose. "Yeah… I might… Well, I dunno. I might like it better if someone else used it other than him."

"Not a fan of the guy?"

She lifted a shoulder. "He's fine. A good person. Funny. A bit of a slacker, though. And he's my… competition. For that job, you know?"

"Got it. No Gin Rummy."

She let out a tiny laugh, her eyes falling to her empty hands now that Robin was busy chewing that bear across the room. Batman snored on the couch above her head.

"You sure have a way with dogs," He pointed to the snoozing pup. "I can't get them to calm down like this."

"I probably make them nervous." She twisted her fingers around the zipper of her jacket. "I tried to ride a horse once, but… Well, the horse could, I dunno, sense my trepidation. It took off before I got within ten feet of it."

He gestured to his very calm for six-month-old puppies. "They hardly look nervous, Gin."

The corner of her mouth lifted. "I like that one."

"Hmm?"

"Gin. You can call me that, if you want."

"All right." He liked it, too. It was short, sweet. Just like her.

He put on a show of flipping out the list, then eyeing her playfully. "One down, twenty-five more to go."

"For now," she said. "I… didn't have time to finish."

"Someone is thorough." He honestly would've been fine simply showing up on Thanksgiving day and proclaiming her his girlfriend without knowing a thing about her, but he had to admit, he was having fun getting to know the girl across the street.

"Favorite color…" he read. The list seemed more like a questionnaire, but he was happy they weren't deeper questions. Like, why are you in love with your ex? "Hmm… Probably orange."

"What do you like about it?" she asked.

He ran a hand over his chin. He'd never been asked that before. "It's nice, I guess. Could be because it's the color of the season right now, though."

"You like colors based on what time of year it is?"

Man, she was getting deep with this simple question. Maybe he'd spoken too soon.

He thought about it, wondering what he would've said two months ago. Would he have picked yellow? Or red? Or brown?

The thought of a pair of beautiful, chocolate brown eyes popped into his mind, and a dull ache burned in his chest. Cassidy's eyes were so dark, they were practically black, and he'd always enjoyed the rich personality they gave her.

No… not brown. Brown couldn't be his favorite. Not dark brown anyway. A light brown… maybe. The light sparkles of a set of honey eyes, so full of curiosity, nervousness, maybe a little shy.

He blinked, shaking his thoughts out of his head. Yeah, that brown would do, but for now… "Nah… I really like orange." He pressed his back up against the couch, sliding down so he could rest his head on the cushion. "Is yours turquoise?"

She turned her head to the side. "Why… why do you think that?"

He flicked the end of her ponytail. "This seems a little bold for you," he teased. "I figured it must be because you really like the color."

Her hand wrapped around her hair, pulling it to the

front where she could see and play with it. "It's pretty," she said. "But it's not my favorite color."

"Orange?" he guessed. "Pink? Purple? Yellow?"

She pursed her lips together, shaking her head as he listed off color after color. He threw his hands in the air when he could've sworn he'd gone through the entire rainbow.

"Don't tell me it's some crazy color no one's heard of except the creators of paint names."

"I'm pretty sure you've heard of green."

"Green!" He smacked his forehead. "I always forget the G in ROY G BIV."

"Lime green, to be specific."

Bright, lime green. He never would've figured such a bright color for such a quiet girl. He liked it.

"Yeah... good call on the blue in the hair instead."

She playfully flipped him in the arm, then almost as if she'd just realized what she'd done, her mouth dropped open slightly, and she snapped her hand back into her lap.

"Um... I... I can't remember what's next."

He grinned at her, his smile having everything to do with the adorable way she played with her zipper and how she not so subtly changed subjects. He let his eyes drift from her to the paper.

"Past relationships..." he said, his voice sinking. The air in the room turned to thick Jell-O. How had she gone from name and favorite color to the hardest question she could ask?

She shyly gazed up from her lap, an apology in her eyes

when they met his. "I… I think… as a girlfriend… I'm supposed to know, right?" She pulled at her ponytail. "That's something people discuss in… serious relationships?"

He stared at the paper, her handwriting blurring, and he quickly wiped his eyes just in case some crap emotion was coming up. A string of barbed wire wrapped around his throat, and he swallowed hard, trying to get rid of the sharp metallic taste of heartache.

"I…" she started, yanking harder on the ends of her hair. "I can go first. Or… if you want… we can come back to that one."

He met her eyes, a soft, caring soul resting in them. She was doing something probably no one else would for a neighborhood friend, and she deserved to know the truth—understand everything and not the cliff notes version he'd blurted out in her kitchen just a few days ago. She was obviously stepping out of some major comfort zones for his sake, and he should return the favor.

He picked at the rug near their thighs, his knuckles occasionally bumping into the stretchy fabric of her running pants. He could talk about Cassidy. He would.

"There's only been one—"

The loud squeak of the screen door cut through his sentence, slicing his courage in half. Jemma's giggles followed immediately after, and Batman and Robin bolted across the floor.

"We're home!" she called out. "So stop macking if you don't want me to make fun of you."

He let out a breathy laugh, meeting Ginny's eyes. She

gave him a small smile. "Later?" she whispered, then her face went bright red. "I mean finish the conversation later. Not… mack…"

Steven leaned in close enough that he could smell fresh laundry and linen on her clothes. "You free Saturday morning?"

ten

The crisp autumn air bit at Ginny's nose as she pushed her hat down over her ears. She tugged at the braided ends hanging from the sides and gave the clouds overhead a wary eye.

"You sure you want to go biking?" she asked Steven. Her biking shorts were a bit on the small side, and when she'd put them on with a pair of knee socks to compensate for the cold, she hadn't counted on rain.

Steven had already straddled his orange bike and was now working on tightening his helmet. How could he look so handsome with that thing on his head?

"The app said we were in for light sprinkles, nothing else." He settled his hands on the handlebars and gave her an encouraging grin. "It won't be a long ride. Promise."

She took a deep breath and propped up on her bicycle. Biking around town was something she was used to, but going up the trail—no matter how tame that trail was—seemed like it might be too much for her little Huffy. Steven had helped her unhook the basket, so it at least looked like it belonged to an adult, but Ginny wobbled the first few pedals down the street, making her feel like five years old and just learning to bike without training wheels. Darn her shaking knees.

Steven led her out of the neighborhood, chatting over the noise of the traffic as they entered into busier territory.

"Feel like asking me any more of those questions?" he asked, twisting around to look at her before concentrating on the road in front of him.

"Um... maybe when we've stopped." She could only do one new thing at a time. As comfortable as she was on a bike, she'd never biked with a partner. Every time he came close to her, she hit the brakes and fell in line behind him. It wasn't the best for conversation, especially for the question she still needed answered from the last time they'd talked.

Even though she was nervous, she was more than willing to tell him about her past relationships—or lack thereof. If he knew she'd never been someone's girlfriend, maybe he'd guide her through what he needed from her on Thanksgiving. Was he going to hold her hand? Would he constantly have his arm around her? Would he... Oh goodness... Would he *kiss* her?

They were all follow-up questions that she needed answers to. If any of those answers were yes, she would need some prep. Maybe some coaching. She couldn't have him reaching for her hand only to have her suddenly rip it from his grasp like he had a clown's buzzer in his palm.

He turned off onto a side road, and she quickly followed, happy to be leaving the busy streets. The neighborhood was well-to-do, with giant houses and gated driveways. Steven pedaled up a hill that Ginny was grateful she had the legs and stamina to follow, even if it wasn't at his inhuman pace, and he stopped at the entrance to a dirt trail.

"You doing all right?" he asked, not an ounce out of breath. Ginny paused, reaching for her water bottle. Rain might not be a bad thing right about now; she could use the cool down.

"I'm... I think so," she said through sips of water. "Are there a lot of hills on the trail?"

He shook his head. "Nah... A little bump here and there. I just want to take you a half mile in. There's a spot I want to show you."

She hoped it was a spot she could sit. She imagined bumping along a dirt trail wasn't going to do her butt any favors.

"O-okay," she said, sliding her water bottle into place. "I'm good."

He pushed onto the trail with barely any effort, and Ginny tried her best to keep up. She really thought she was in better shape than this. Biking to and from work five times a week had given her a pair of toned calves, but they were doing nothing for her now. Her muscles ached as the bumps Steven led her on pushed them to their limits. She was proud she only had to stop once at the bottom of one of those hills and give herself a pep talk before attempting it.

A quarter mile in, the trail leveled and they pedaled into a nice open field where a group of well-toned and bulky guys huddled in the distance.

Dirt flew up on the path in front of her as Steven slammed on his brakes. Ginny had to swerve to avoid smacking into his back tire.

"What... Are you okay?" she asked, turning around to

meet his eyes. He stared off at the field, watching the group of future NFL players break from the huddle and get into formation. The quarterback's deep voice filled the air as he called out the play, and the slamming of skin on skin snapped and echoed around them.

Steven dismounted, letting his bike hit the dirt. He gave her a mischievous grin that sent her stomach into a frenzy.

"Let's play."

She jerked back. "Um... Excuse me?"

He marched toward her, his hands careful as he unclicked her helmet. "Come on. Let's play some football."

He wanted her to what now? "With them?" she choked out. "No, no... they're playing tackle. I'm... I don't even know... What if they're practicing or something?"

"Well, it's worth an ask, right?" He dragged his hand down her arm, leaving goosebumps in his wake, then gently tugged on her wrist. The frantic butterflies in her belly were too busy flying into each other for her to appreciate how wonderful it felt to be touched like that.

"And with a gorgeous girl like you asking, I doubt they'll say no."

Dizziness set in. "You want me... I have to ask them?"

"We're working on your confidence, yeah?" He was far too calm for this. She wasn't even sure if she was breathing. "What better way to start?"

She could think of a billion better ways to start that didn't involve talking to a group of very attractive guys she was going to have to play a *tackle sport* with if they said yes. That was if she even got the words to leave her mouth.

Her heart thudded in her ears, pounding to the beat of the *Jaws* theme song. Steven still had his hand wrapped around her wrist, but he could've been a figment of her imagination for all she knew. Her vision tunneled, and she stopped in her tracks, pleading with her eyes to him. *Please don't make me do this. Don't make me talk to them. Please let me go back in my safe shell.*

He focused on her, his playful grin disappearing into a line of concern. His blue eyes softened, and he stepped to her. He tentatively cupped her cheeks, his touch so gentle she wasn't even sure he was actually in contact with her.

His eyes held such care that her breathing started to calm, her heart slowing to its regular pace.

"You don't have to," he said, his voice low and comforting, the dimples in his cheeks less prominent but still peeking from the shadows. "I want to help, Gin. I know you can do this, but only if you want to." His hands slowly dropped from her cheeks, cold air replacing them. He held onto her shoulders, rubbing them with comforting circles. "Take a deep breath, think about what you want for yourself, and then you decide. Whatever it is, I'll go along with it."

His voice was a shot of morphine. She could already feel her body relaxing with the low comfort of his words. His hands massaged that relaxation into her skin, and she felt it seep into her muscles and wash over her bones. She locked eyes with him, focusing on the depths of those ocean blues as she inhaled deeply through her nose. She held it there for a moment, then blew it out, his black hair fluttering from her breath.

What she wouldn't give to have the courage to walk up to those guys and ask to join their game. She knew the rules; that wasn't a problem.

Then what was the problem?

She searched her body, her heart only jolting a little with the idea of crossing the field and opening her mouth. She couldn't trust her voice to come out strong, but she could trust her legs to carry her over there.

She held Steven's eyes, losing herself in the calm soul that lived behind them. He wanted to help her, and he didn't even know the whole story. He had no clue how much she wanted to overcome her fears so she could help others with theirs. No idea that she needed the money to afford that schooling. He simply said okay. Yes, she was doing something for him, but in comparison, his job was going to be so much harder than hers.

"Will you…" she started, then took another deep breath before finishing. "Will you hold my hand? While I ask, I mean."

The corner of his mouth picked up, and the dimple in his right cheek cratered. "Absolutely."

He slid his hand over her shoulder, trailing it down to her elbow and forearm. She swallowed hard, staying stone still as he settled his fingers between each of hers, their palms kissing.

She'd never held hands with a guy like this. Once upon a time her former dates would try, but there were never so slow, so careful, so comforting or intimate. Ginny took the first step toward the football players, her heart a nice, calming beat. It was the strangest sensation to be holding hands with someone and feel so anchored to her own world. Almost as if Steven belonged in there with her.

They crossed the open field in what felt like seconds, but Ginny knew it had to have been much longer. Steven held onto her, never letting go.

They waited on the sidelines while the guys ran the next play. Ginny bounced up and down on her heels, nibbling on the inside of her lip, contemplating on heading back to their bikes a few thousand times, but Steven would squeeze her hand, reminding her that she had a life goal, and she'd never reach it if she stayed hidden.

The players hit a break, and Ginny cleared her throat, hoping her voice came out loud enough to the tall wide receiver walking past.

"That was... um... a really great catch," she said. The guy stopped, gazing at her over his shoulder. She could feel her heart beat in her temples.

"Thanks." His eyes fell to their joined hands before coming back up to meet hers. "You a fan of the game?"

She'd grown up in a house of football fanatics, and she was known to be at the occasional Huskies game. "We were... I mean, I was wondering..." *Here it goes.* Steven squeezed her hand again, and a tidal wave of courage sprang up in her chest. "Do you guys have room for two more?"

The wide receiver raised his brows. "You wanna play?"

She nodded, unable to trust her voice to say anything else. The guy quirked a grin and shouted to his buddies. "Anyone up for a touch game?"

A few guys peered over, and they got about ten volunteers ready to keep going. The rest all took a spot on the grass with their waters and sports drinks.

"You know the rules?" the guy asked Steven and Ginny—mostly Ginny. She nodded again, a smile growing on her face. Were they actually going to play?

"All right." He turned to the rest of the team. "We got our two captains here! Touch rules! First to twenty-one wins!"

Ginny's eyes widened, and she shot a look at Steven. He lifted a shoulder and eased his hand out of hers. "Guess we're playing against each other." He leaned in and whispered. "Take it easy on me, okay?"

A wave of playfulness hit her, and she wasn't sure where it came from, but she said it anyway. "Not a chance, love pumpkin."

Her boldness was rewarded with the sexiest laugh she'd ever heard. If she could get something like that every time she showed a bit of courage, maybe she would open her mouth more often.

eleven

Steven wiped his forehead free of sweat and took his position in the line-up. Score was fourteen to fourteen. Fourth and goal. He was defending, and Ginny was ready to run for the opposing team. He knew they'd throw to her; she'd impressed every single one of the players, himself included, by how many passes she'd caught. Steven found himself thinking less and less about how fake their relationship was and more and more about how real it felt.

The quarterback called the play, and the center hiked the ball. Ginny took off along the right side, and Steven ran over to intercept. She was fast, but no match for him. He blocked, and she smacked into his chest.

His hands fell to her waist, and a giggle slipped from her smiling lips. She wiggled in his hold, which only tightened. Damn, she was stronger than she looked, and with adrenaline fueling her, she wasn't shy about calling him out on cheating.

"This is touch football, not hug football, Steven!" she giggled in his ear. She twisted in his hold like one of the frantic kittens at the shelter. "Holding! I call holding!"

A bubble formed around them, fuzzing the sounds of the game and blurring the field. She smelled of lavender and fresh cut grass, and her laughter was a bright light in the middle of the cloudy day. Her body bumped against his, her long ponytail hitting him in the face as she squirmed.

"You're not getting this one," he teased. She spun in his arms and smacked at his fists. He felt her sliding down his body, her slim frame wriggling to a crouch. His sweaty fingers lost their grip, and he tossed his head back as she crawled through his legs and scrambled to her feet.

The ball found its way to her open hands, and she danced across the goal line, playfully sticking her tongue out at him. Wait a damn minute… Was that the same girl he'd come here with?

He settled his hands on his hips as he caught his breath. That was the game, and the shy girl from across the street had made every touchdown for her team. He was ashamed to admit how surprised he felt—he hadn't been sure she'd last the first fifteen minutes of the game, let alone own with all the experienced players.

"We get her next time," Scott, one of the players on his team called out right as Walker, the quarterback for Ginny's team slammed into her and hoisted her over his shoulder. Her face was a bright red tomato, lighting up the field. Walker jogged her up and down the goal line, pumping his fist in the air. Nervous laughter escaped Ginny in tune with each bounce, and something twisted in Steven's gut, his eyes laser focused on Walker's hand around Ginny's bare thighs. Her pink bike shorts showed off more than she'd probably bargained for, and Steven covered the ten yards to the goal line in less than a second.

"All right, all right… put her down."

Walker spun her around, and the look on her face was utter terror mixed with forced amusement. Steven was ready to knock the guy one in the gut, but he set Ginny on the grass and let out a celebratory holler. He ran past Steven, acting like a complete buffoon, and Steven locked eyes with Ginny.

"Okay…?" he asked. She adjusted her shorts and fixed her messed ponytail. A rock of guilt plopped into his stomach for wrestling with her on the field just a moment ago, and he prayed he hadn't made her this uncomfortable.

"Yes… I'm… It was a little…" She leaned in, dropping her voice to a whisper. "You didn't see my butt, did you?"

He winced playfully. "Well…"

Her eyes widened in horror, and he quickly took it back.

"I'm kidding, Gin." He chuckled and tentatively swung an arm around her shoulders. Her tense stance relaxed under his touch, and she slowly lifted her arm to wrap around his waist.

They said a quick goodbye and thank you to the guys, who invited them to join in the Turkey Bowl on Thanksgiving morning. They had other plans, but Steven wasn't going to call the shots. Ginny was running this show.

"You still okay to ride to the place I wanted to show you? It's not too much farther," he asked, pulling on his helmet. Ginny swung her leg over her bike and nodded. She was awfully quiet, and Steven didn't want to prod, but it was killing him. Had he pushed her too far? She seemed to be having fun until she was swung over a shoulder and paraded about like a trophy. He shook his hands out before placing them on his bike grips. He adjusted gears and started toward Echo Rock—a name he'd given a spot just off the bike trail. He'd ask her there, or when they rode back into town, if she was truly okay. If playing football had helped. If he shouldn't touch her like he had…

About five minutes later, he spotted the turnoff and eased to a stop, Ginny following close behind. She gave him a small smile, hopping off her bike and pushing out the kickstand.

"Is… I mean, are we here?"

He gestured up through a few trees. "Just through there."

"Our bikes will be okay?" she asked, hanging her helmet on her handlebar. She pulled her woolen hat out from her jacket pocket and pulled it onto her head.

"Hopefully," he teased. His eyes dropped to her twisting hands, and he held out his palm. *She doesn't have to take it*, he told himself. But a warm trickle of relief sank through his chest when she did.

He led her through the rough terrain, his new shoes slipping on the wet leaves and rocks, his hand buzzing from her touch. As the trees thinned, they stood on a precipice overlooking a field of rocks and leaves. She stopped in her tracks, pulling on his arm.

"I… Sorry, I don't do… heights very well."

"That's okay." He backed up, standing next to her a safe twenty feet from the edge. "It'll still work from here."

Curiosity wrinkled her forehead and painted her large,

honey-colored eyes. "What will… I mean, what are we doing?"

The corner of his mouth lifted, and he turned toward the rocks below. He used to come here after school and tell the cliff all his secrets. They'd echo back at him, so not only was he getting everything off his chest, he could hear it out loud more than once.

He thought it would be perfect for her—get out some of the stuff she never said.

"Yell."

She jerked back. "What?"

"Yell over the edge. Tell those rocks whatever you want."

Her face went blank, and she stared up at him with those honey eyes, her mouth open as she lifted her shoulders.

His heart hit his chest, thick and heavy. He supposed he was asking a lot, especially from someone so shy. He wasn't shy whatsoever, yet it was hard for him to shout out in front of her. Maybe he didn't want to scare her, or maybe he wasn't sure he was ready to drag her so deeply into his baggage. But he'd eventually have to; her list of questions were bound to come up again.

He took a deep breath and faced the rocks again. "I'm in love with my ex!" he shouted into the void. His voice slapped against the stone and rustled the leaves, the echoes floating around them in surround sound. His admission was stated at least four times before it melted into the sounds of nature.

He slowly turned to her, shame curling his lip downward. She kept hold of his hand, her fingers slightly twitching. Her eyes were nothing but concern and sorrow—far more than he deserved.

"You wanted to know about my past relationships?" he said. "That's the only one that matters."

The wind picked her hair up and swung it around her face underneath her hat. His shoulders drooped in disappointment, shame, sadness... He stared at their joined hands, wondering why she hadn't let him go. Did she know just how much he needed someone to anchor him?

"We were high school sweethearts," he started. "Cassidy was this complete nerd—still is—and I loved it. She was fun and silly, and said the most random things. We were each other's firsts with everything... including heartbreaks."

Ginny stepped in closer, hanging onto his every word. He appreciated how well she kept eye contact, especially since he knew her well enough to know eye contact made her uncomfortable. The urge to run a hand over her face suddenly took over, and he settled for sweeping her turquoise and brown hair over her shoulder.

"I knew when I applied to school in Boston, that would be it. Long distance wasn't going to work—it would only make us hate each other in the end. That's what I told myself; it's what I believed. I broke it off, telling her I wanted to remain friends, but I never fell out of love. Not through other relationships, not through distance... Nothing could shake Cassidy. I came back home a few months ago...

for her."

The words fell from his lips, taking with them the weight they'd carried. The tension in his chest felt lighter, his head less foggy, and his gaze dropped to Ginny's lips as she ran a tongue over them. Her fingers squeezed his, and he managed a sad smile.

"Now I'm too late. She's got someone. And I'm… stuck." He let out a hollow laugh. "I already hate the guy. Haven't met him, don't know him, don't care. I hate him."

Her shoulders shook with silent amusement. She slowly turned to the overlook, the wind blowing her hair and waving her loose jacket. He was reminded of a painting he'd seen from a street artist in Boston. A gorgeous woman's profile, blue hair blowing around her, the sun casting every color of the rainbow across her fair skin.

She took in a deep breath and blew it out slowly. "I'm…" she started softly. "I'm jealous."

"What?"

Her lips pursed, and she took another breath. "I'm jealous!" she shouted over the edge, her voice strained like she'd never been this loud in her life. It echoed back to her, and a smile wrapped on her lips, blush rushing through her cheeks.

"I'm so freaking jealous!" she said again, this time with a laugh. The air cleared around him, and he joined in her amusement.

"Feel good?" he asked, and she nodded, her voice continuing to echo around them. "What are you jealous of?"

"Everyone. Everything." She let out a happy sigh and

gazed up at the clouds. "Lauren for her passion. Ashlynn for her lack of inhibitions. Jemma for her confidence. Alex for his charisma. You."

His mouth turned upward. "What about me?"

Her eyes fell to his. "Your honesty."

He snorted. "I'm not that good at honesty. I haven't told Cassidy how I feel."

"But you... you're honest with yourself." She lifted a shoulder. "I think you'd be surprised with how many people aren't."

He let that sink in, a shocking swell of pride swooping through him. He was used to being called the nice guy—good ol' reliable Steven. It felt different to be viewed as something else entirely. Good.

"I... I had fun today," she said after a moment.

"Even with Walker..."

She bit away a laugh. "Well, yes... I just... I really thought I was mooning everyone." She let go of his hand, pulled at her shorts, and tugged her knee socks up. "But I really did have... you know... fun. So... T-thank you."

Cold replaced her touch, and he pushed his hands into his pockets. His ego was certainly blown to capacity, and he smiled to himself. "Anytime, love pumpkin."

twelve

Ginny shifted on her bed, her legs burning from her laptop. She lay on her stomach, pushing the computer up on a pillow. A fuzzy brown three-year-old pup with the cutest blue eyes she'd ever seen—with one exception—stared at her through the screen, practically begging her to come visit. But she knew if she did, she'd adopt the dog in a second.

She ran her forefinger over the dwindling image of the bike on her wrist. She owed that dog big time; she never would've gotten the courage to agree to help Steven if Cocoa hadn't been nuzzling her. The soft fur and warm breath of the sweet little dog had been a comfort she wasn't too familiar with, but she was learning to recognize the feeling. The ghost touch of Steven's hand in hers was still lingering against her palm, even though she hadn't seen him in twenty-four hours.

Her nails traced the lines in her palm, her mind skating from Cocoa to her Saturday morning. Her eyelids fluttered closed as she remembered the feel of his hands around her waist, his manly scent, his dimples… They were all qualities that should've had her running, tail between her legs, nerves buzzing to the point of combustion. But Steven had the opposite effect on her. She wasn't nervous with him; he was comfort in a bottle.

A very handsome bottle.

Did a person count as an emotional support animal?

Her head lifted, a light clicking on in the corner of her mind. Could that work? The clubhouse rules were strict for a reason, but there had to be exceptions. An emotional support animal just might be one of them.

Cocoa definitely fit the bill. She was a calming fuzzball. Ginny imagined life a little less scary with a furry friend by her side.

She tapped her nails against her laptop, gathering the courage to grab her phone and text Steven—check to see if Cocoa was even still available.

Morning! Wait... delete. It was well after noon. *Hey! How are you?*

She sent it off, bounding her foot off her mattress while she waited for his response. The bubbles appeared and knotted her stomach with excitement. She was doing it—initiating conversation.

Save me, he sent. Then a picture loaded underneath of two adorable puppies sitting on his face, their tails wagging so hard they were blurred in the photo. She bit away her smile and brought both hands up to her phone.

Such vicious creatures.

And they're getting fat, he quickly responded. *Jemma keeps feeding them under the table.*

Who can blame her? Look at those faces.

He texted back with another picture, this one of Batman with his tongue hanging out the side of his mouth, his face awfully close to Steven's while Robin's butt rested on Steven's ear. His bright blue eyes were wide with faux annoyance. It was hardly fair that any one man could be that beautiful and that nice.

Ginny quickly bat down the giddiness erupting in her stomach. He was in love with someone else, and she was a stand-in. It was okay; it was what she agreed to. So her heart could not go falling for the boy across the street, even if he was sort of perfect.

Are you going to be at work tomorrow? she asked, needing to get to her point of messaging him in the first place.

Bright and early. Did you wanna get together after work? Finish that list of questions ;)

She still had plenty of those. At least they had hand holding down already.

I was actually wondering if you could see if Cocoa was still available for adoption.

Her message hung out there without a response for a good five minutes. Maybe he was checking on it for her. He didn't have to do that on his day off, but he seemed just the guy who would. He carried a whole gallon of milk across town for her, after all.

The doorbell rang through the house, and Ginny perked her head up, moving her phone and laptop to peer down the hall. Lauren was in the living room, fully engrossed in one of her self-help books that she read every Sunday while her boyfriend sat on his phone, but she was aware enough to answer the door.

"Hey. Lauren, right? Is Ginny around?" Steven's voice floated through the house, and Ginny scrambled up, ripping her hair from her scraggly ponytail and quickly dragging her fingers through it. She snatched up a pillow and hugged it to her chest, knowing there was no way she could get a bra on before he was walking down the hallway.

"Yeah. She's straight down the hall. Pretty sure she's awake."

She was awake all right. Sunday naps were usually the staple of the clubhouse girls, but sleep hadn't found her today.

She pulled her laptop in front of her, faking casual as Steven's heavy steps echoed down the hall.

"Knock, knock," he said, rapping her doorframe with his knuckle. She was not going to get distracted by his mussed black hair, his piercing blue eyes, the plaid button-down that opened to a Batman logo tee, or his nice jeans that clung tight and spoke volumes to how much the guy walked, jogged, or biked everywhere he went.

"H-hey." Her lips curled up in what she hoped was a smile, but she really wasn't sure. Steven had a close-up view of her bedroom, and it wasn't exactly clean. She made sure not to shoot her gaze to her underwear hanging out of the laundry basket.

He nodded to the empty spot on her full-size bed. "You mind?"

She shook her head, her breath and heart stopping a full twenty seconds as his weight dipped her mattress. He slid up the scrunched comforter and thousands of pillows, settling in on his elbow next to her. She made sure her pillow was still covering her chest. She was a no bra kind of girl, especially in big sweater weather.

His dimple deepened when he caught the website she was on. "I took that picture of her last week when you visited. She was a lot friendlier that day than usual."

"Really?" She frowned, scrolling through Cocoa's profile. "She was so sweet."

"She is, but she's spooked. Poor girl got dropped off by her family and put up for adoption. I think it's starting to sink in that they aren't coming back for her, so she's down most of the time. And when people come in to see her, they pass right on by because of how badly she shakes. A lot of nervous pets bite, so you know, parents with little kids get a little wary of her. And the playful pups get chosen first."

He spoke like it didn't bother him, but there was a sadness that deepened the lines in his forehead. Ginny had picked up on that trait of his here and there over the course of the week.

"So..." he said, adjusting on the bed, relaxing into it like it were his own. His toned arms tucked under his head, and Ginny shot her gaze to the computer so she didn't gawk at his impressive triceps. "Do you know someone who might want her?"

"Um... Sorry... What?" Her brain was fuzz. What was wrong with her? Steven was her comfort, but him in her bed was throwing her off—and not in a bad way either. It wasn't discomfort she felt, but more of a growing ache she wasn't sure how to satisfy.

Steven rolled to his side, facing her dead on. "You asked if she was still up for adoption."

"Oh… right." She shook herself out of her head and focused. "I was actually… Well, I was thinking that maybe I could…"

Her voice trailed off, and she let him finish her sentence in his head.

"I thought you girls had a no pets rule."

"We do. But… Well, I was going to ask about… an emotional support animal. Maybe. If that would be… you know, okay."

His brows lifted, and he sat up straighter on the pillows so he was eye level with her. "You think they'd be all right with that?"

Excitement painted his tone and latched onto her heart. "I hope so. There's no harm in asking, I guess."

"For sure." He motioned to her computer screen. "She'd be the perfect support animal for you, and vice versa."

A confused laugh fell from her lips. She tilted her head, and he grinned.

"You were good for her, is all I'm saying. She spends most of her days huddled in the corner of her kennel. When you were around, she was jumping, cuddling, sleeping without trembling."

Huh… maybe humans *could* be support animals. "Could I see her tomorrow?" she asked. "I don't want it to be… like a fluke or something."

"Sure. She does her exercises around noon, four, and then later at seven. But I get off at five, so come before then."

"You want to see me, too?" she teased, shocking herself with her boldness.

"Always," he said playfully. He closed his eyes and settled into her pillows. "Man, how do you leave this room? My mattress isn't nearly this comfortable."

She let out a small laugh, shutting her laptop and easing down next to him. Her arms wrapped tight around the pillow, keeping it on lockdown against her chest as she rolled to face him.

"I spoiled myself last tax season," she said, patting the mattress with her foot. "Twelve-inch memory foam."

"Who knew heaven was at Mattress Warehouse?"

She nervously grinned, letting her eyes skate over him while he cozied up in her pillows and comforter. She could never be so brave, though she amused herself with the idea of knocking on his door, jumping onto his mattress, and sinking into his sheets. Batman and Robin were sure to join them, bouncing playfully around their legs before settling in for a puppy nap.

She imagined an orange and gray color scheme, wondering if he painted or decorated using his favorite color. Lots of dog fur, even if he had vacuumed earlier, more puzzles hanging on the wall. Maybe a picture or two of him with his grandma or parents.

Did he have parents?

He popped an eye open, startling her from her thoughts. Half his mouth perked up at the side. "Do I have something on my face?"

"How..." She paused, sinking into her pillows. Her

fingers reached for her thick, leafy printed quilt, and she covered herself, finally giving the chest pillow some time off. "How are you so comfortable… with… well, being you?"

She wasn't sure how else to phrase it without pointing out the obvious—that he was in her bed, almost napping, and he didn't even seem the slightest bit nervous about it.

A breathy laugh escaped him. "I'm not so sure I am."

"You are," she argued, picking at a tie in the quilt. "You're… Well, you're in my bed, aren't you?"

He turned his head on the pillow, opening both eyes to meet hers. She stopped herself from looking away.

"Is it okay that I'm here?" he asked, genuinely concerned.

"Yes," she said. "I'm only saying… It would be hard for me. To lie in someone else's bed."

"Anyone else's?"

She nodded. She'd only sat on the edge of Lauren's once. She'd been too nervous to enter rooms that weren't hers.

A long, deep breath filled the room, and she watched Steven's chest go up and down with the movement. His head turned toward the ceiling, and his eyes closed again.

"I'm not that bold, either, to tell you the truth. But it's kinda easy with you. Maybe Cocoa's picking up on that, you know? It's comfortable around you."

"Me?" There was absolutely no way she could be the calming spirit. She was barely calm when she was just around herself.

"Mmmhmm," he said, his voice dropping, almost as if

he was going to zonk out at any moment. She wasn't the least bit tired, but she wasn't as frantic as she thought she'd be in a situation like this.

"Steven?" she asked, her voice soft but strong. "Are you planning on... kissing me at the dinner?"

He swiveled toward her, his eyes fluttering open like he was forcing them. "Maybe a peck or something. Is that okay?"

She loved that he always asked. "Could you... I don't know... define a peck?"

His dimple twitched, and he pushed up on his elbow to face her. "Soft. Quick. No tongue." He laughed, but a shot of nerves went straight through her, and she couldn't find it in her to join him. "If it's a problem, I'll put it on the cheek."

That was a little more comforting, but disappointment hit her, and she pulled at her bottom lip. "O-okay. I just... Well, you should probably know that I've never..." She held her breath, counting in her head, berating herself to just blurt it out already. But the image of the shock she knew she'd see on his face was humiliating. Her cheeks were already running warm at just the thought.

No, she couldn't say it. She didn't want to.

But just as she was about to tell him to forget it, realization dawned in his eyes.

"You've never been kissed?"

Her face lit up like a firecracker, and she buried into her quilt, shaking her head. "It's humiliating, I know," her voice muffled into the thick fabric. Steven's laughter floated over her head, making the heat in her face ten thousand degrees hotter.

"It's not," he said, his hand landing on her shoulder. He rubbed up and down the quilt, creating havoc in her belly. "Gin, I haven't been kissed either."

She peered out from the quilt. "Really?"

He snorted, tossing his head back. "Gin, I'm teasing you. I'm in love with my ex, remember? Of course I've kissed other people."

Her embarrassment quickly turned into playful rage, and she grabbed a pillow and swung it at his head. "Buttface!" she bit out.

"Buttface? You call me buttface?"

"Yes!" She smacked him again with the pillow, laughter on the edges of her voice. She caught a glimpse of that Batman logo on his shirt and started singing the tune to the theme song, replacing "Batman" with "Buttface."

He swiped the pillow and stuffed it under his bum, laughing as he fought her for more ammo. He managed to get all the pillows underneath him, and Ginny sunk into the mattress in defeat.

"You spoil all my fun," she teased. It was miles from the truth. Steven stretched over all the pillows, letting out a long, relaxed sigh.

"Ahhhhhh."

She backhanded him lightly in the shoulder, then crossed her arms and stared at the ceiling. Her heart was on fire, buzzing with adrenaline and freedom. How did he do that? How did he release this person inside of her? No one else seemed to have the key.

She twisted her hands, riding the high of the pillow fight. "I don't mind," she said, her voice a lot more breathy than she anticipated.

"What's that?"

She turned to face him, using up the entire dosage of courage he'd just given her. "I don't mind if you kiss me on Thanksgiving."

His playful grin slowly faded, replaced with a concerned frown. He pulled a pillow out from under him and snugged it under her head.

"Your first kiss shouldn't be for show," he said quietly.

"But... You've done so much for me already. I want to do my part."

"Gin..."

"I'm okay with it." And she was. It wasn't like she was saving her first kiss or anything. It was simply the opportunity had never arose. Nerves had always gotten the better of her, and she tugged at the inside of her lip briefly before going on. "But... I think... Well, I might need a... run through first."

He sighed. "Like a dress rehearsal?"

She frowned, catching onto his lack of enthusiasm. Maybe he was just trying to let her down easy. Of course he didn't *want* to kiss her. He was in love with someone else, so the kiss would be completely for show. So kissing her beforehand wasn't something he was excited about.

"But it's okay. I mean, we can just do the cheek thing if that's what you want. I'm not like, trying to get you to kiss me or anything, I was just saying if you come in for a 'peck' on Thanksgiving, I might not know what to do. I might not be able to sell it for you, and I know you want this so bad so I want to give my all for it—"

He reached for her cheeks, and her words snapped off. His hands were firm but gentle on her skin, lighting up every nerve ending in her body. Her breath was somewhere in the air around them, and she wondered if it'd come back down before she passed out.

He kept her close, waiting for her breathing to return. His eyes searched hers, and she wondered what he found. Could he see how much she enjoyed this proximity as much as she was terrified of it? Could he see her nerves dancing with her excitement? His thumb traced a pattern across her jawline, and she slid off the pillow under her head, using him as her cushion.

"It'll be short," he said, his words sweet warmth against her mouth. "Very quick. Maybe less than a second."

"O-okay."

"And we'll be standing." The corner of his mouth twitched. She allowed herself a breathy laugh, her head dipping slightly before leveling back with his mouth. "I'll put my hand on your waist." He dropped one of his palms and wrapped his gentle fingers around her hip. He squeezed the thick fabric of her quilt and shot liquid heat through her lower abdomen.

"O-okay."

"Don't worry about doing anything," he assured her. "I'll lean down and find your lips." His forehead pressed against hers, and she gulped, her chin trembling under his thumb. His eyes burned into hers, never leaving, always searching.

"Are you all right?" he whispered. She nodded against his forehead. Her eyes eased shut. Her heart was a hummingbird about to burst from its home and take on the world of sweet nectar. She parted her lips even though she knew enough to know that a peck didn't require an open mouth. But if she didn't, she'd suffocate with how little air she seemed to be getting.

"Are you... okay that it's me?" he asked, his lips brushing hers ever so slightly.

She nodded again, her voice cracking when she answered with a small, "Yes."

He hesitated, long enough for her to take in every sensation—his hand on her hip, his thumb on her chin, the quiet of the clubhouse and the raucous of her heart. Her hands wound tight in the quilt, not knowing where to go or what to touch. She longed to reach out and run her fingers along his smooth jawline or caress the feather-soft look of his hair. But her nerves froze her in place, and her excitement allowed Steven to press his lips against hers.

Her heart flew into her throat, and what was meant to be less than a second turned into a lifetime. His grip on her hip tightened, and she slid into him, her body zipping with his. Her fingers loosened from the quilt and feathered to his neck, gently smoothing over his skin while his mouth worked magic on hers. There was no worrying over whether or not she was doing it right; with the way her body electrified, she no longer cared about anything but his touch and how it made her feel. Sensations she never knew possible popped and exploded like a shaken up Coke can. It felt like all the time in the world and no time at all before it fizzled out.

His lips left hers with a soft pop, and she instinctively let out a content whimper. Her cheeks would've probably been bright red if they hadn't already been up in smoke.

Her eyes fluttered open, meeting his. A thick stone of worry plopped into her stomach. Had she been okay? Did she do it right?

His hand skated up her hip and pushed back the hair that had fallen over her cheek. He gave her a playful nose wrinkle.

"You're a natural."

"Really?"

He dropped her cheeks, slowly settling on his back. He tucked his hand behind his head, the other resting on his abs. "Yep. No need to be nervous about it."

"Okay," she said, the high from his kiss starting to melt with his nonchalance. "That's... good."

Silence crept over them like a storm cloud, and when his breathing leveled to a sleepy rhythm, she curled into her quilt and shut her eyes.

Of course he was going to be indifferent. She wasn't anything but a girlfriend for hire, essentially, and a first-time kisser wouldn't compare to the love of his life, but she hoped for some kind of reaction from him.

She shook her head free from negative thoughts and decided to pat herself on the back instead. If she'd told her past self that she'd be in bed with the boy across the street, letting him sleep after kissing her, her past self would've laughed in her face.

That job was in the bag if she kept this up. She only had to remember not to fall for Steven in the process, which was proving harder and harder to do.

thirteen

Steven looked at the clock for fifth time in the past ten minutes. He swore the hands weren't even moving. Time was simply stuck at half past three, and he was stuck in an endless loop of jitters.

Ginny was supposedly dropping by soon to meet up with Cocoa, and even though Steven knew she wasn't going to be there to see him, he'd been bouncing around the shelter as if *he* was the one getting the visitor.

He ducked behind one of the desks to check his phone so the boss didn't give him grief about it. His messages were frustratingly all old, but that didn't stop him from scrolling through the conversation he'd had with her last night. When he'd roused from the impromptu nap at her house the day before, she was out like a light, her breath softly blowing the loose strands of her hair. She'd clung to that thick quilt like it was a teddy bear, and he'd sat for a moment just watching her lips, her shoulders move up and down, her content expression…

All he hoped was that he hadn't taken away something very special. It seemed a shame to wait so long for a first kiss to only have it with someone who was using her to keep face. But something had taken over him when he lied next to her, and he suddenly was so sick of being the nice guy. He wanted to be a little selfish.

Movement flickered in his peripheral, and he pushed his phone into his pocket and greeted the family with a smile.

"Hello. What can I do for you?"

"We'd like to look at the dogs," the woman said, swinging her joined hand with her son back and forth. The kid was probably around seven or eight, and his eager eyes peered around Steven to the barking in the back.

"Sure thing," he said. "Just need a driver's license and car keys if you plan on taking any of them outside for a bit."

"Okay," the mom said, and then he led them back to the pups. The boy walked right up to Cocoa's kennel, peering in with wondering eyes.

Steven's heart stuttered, and he about told them that Cocoa was being considered for adoption with someone else, but the boy looked up at his mom and shook his head.

"That one is boring," he said, and Steven held back a laugh. As soon as the kid and his mom moved on to look at the others, Steven stepped up to Cocoa's door.

"Hey, girl," he said. She huddled in the corner, shaking. Her eyes drooped, her ears back, and her tail tucked underneath her. If there were awards for the saddest dog alive, he was sure she'd have it in the bag.

Steven frowned and eyed the clock again. It was still too early to take her out, but he didn't care. The poor girl needed some fresh air.

He headed out front to make sure there was someone to help the mom and the boy when they were ready, and then grabbed a leash and some doggie treats.

"Cocoa," he said, opening her kennel slowly. "Look what I got for you, girl."

The pup barely lifted her head at the treat. She sniffed the air, but with a sad sigh, she settled back against her paws, uninterested.

Steven's gaze fell to the untouched food dish in the corner.

"Not hungry today, huh?" he asked, jingling the leash instead. "What about a walk?"

With some coaxing, he got her to at least let him hook the leash on and carry her to the exercise yard. She shivered in his arms, her little heart beat pounding under his hand. Maybe today wasn't the best day for Ginny to visit. Cocoa was more depressed than normal; she didn't move a muscle when he set her in the grass.

"What's got you so nervous?" he mused, crouching next to her. He stuck his hand out to stroke the soft fur over her head, but she jerked away from him and walked on a set of shaky legs to the corner of the fence. She pushed her face against the chain link, her fur poking through as a soft whine escaped.

Steven frowned, straightening his stance. He toyed with the leash, clicking the latch. What would her previous owners think about this? Would they have dumped her and ran if they'd known how depressed she'd be?

He pulled his phone out and sent a message to the shelter vet. It might be time for a check-up—make sure it wasn't anything else.

The door to the exercise area squeaked open, and Steven whipped his head around, a smile in place to greet Ginny, but it was a different set of brown eyes that met his.

"Hey," he said, his smile fading into confusion. Cassidy fixed her glasses and waved, eyeing the grass and avoiding any poop on her way over. "What are you doing here?" he asked.

"Haven't heard from you in like a week," she said, hopping over a questionable spot of grass. "Making sure you're still alive."

"Phone goes both ways, Cass," he teased, but his tone tasted off, like he'd bitten into something sweet and gotten sour.

"I know, I know. It's been crazy around work. We got a few new people back in billing and training them has been exhausting. But thank Thor they aren't idiots. I think they'll be good to go after Thanksgiving."

He internally snorted. Cassidy was always taking Thor's name in vein, and back when they were together, it would lead into another argument over what was better: Marvel or DC. Well, he had two labs at home that would forever back up his DC love.

"So… speaking of Thanksgiving," Cassidy continued, tilting her head. Her messy bun jostled with the movement, and with her glasses she looked like a librarian scolding kids for being too loud. It was part of her charm, and a sense of loss washed over him so unexpectedly he had to look away from her.

"Still planning on it."

"You'd better be," she said with a laugh. "But... you said your girlfriend was, like, a good baker or something?"

Damn, he had said that, hadn't he. "Why...?"

She gave him a look. "Come on... You know my mom's pie is a goopy mess of pumpkin mix and whipped cream."

A chuckle rose from his gut before he could stop it. The memory of Grandpa's face last year when he'd dug into the pie and got an unexpected taste was the funniest thing about the evening. And there wasn't a chance of Cassidy's mom leaving the room, either, so Grandpa discreetly scooped glops of it into his napkin then offered to clean the table.

"Good times," he mused. "But I take it you want an edible dessert?"

"Obviously." Cassidy would eat pie for every meal if given the opportunity. The girl had not just one sweet tooth, but an entire mouthful of them. "You think your girl could make me a pumpkin pie that I can actually eat?"

He had no clue if Ginny was capable of making pie. The only baking experience he'd had with her was with a pan full of burnt cookies. If that was any indication, it wasn't looking good.

Cocoa suddenly jerked awake from the fence, her ears perked, her tail slowly moving into a wag. Steven's brow furrowed, and he followed the dog's line of sight to the empty doorway.

"What're you looking at, girl?" he asked the dog. Cassidy turned around, a small smile twitching in the corner of her mouth.

"Probably her," she said, and Cocoa took off. Steven shot his gaze back to the doors, and Ginny stood just outside of them, eyes swiveling between Steven and Cassidy.

Cocoa's tail went wild, and Ginny dropped her eyes to the dog and smiled. She crouched down, meeting the pup with a good head scratch and praises of how good a girl she was.

"Well," Steven said, starting toward Ginny, "you can ask her about the pies yourself."

A slow smile spread across Cassidy's face. "Is this your girlfriend?"

Ginny lifted her head, her eyes big and scared. Cocoa kept jumping at her, the most alive he'd seen the dog all day.

"Um…" Ginny said softly, wrapping her hands under the dog's belly and pulling her up from the ground. "Yeah… t-that's me."

A protective wave hit him, and the urge to blanket her in safety pushed him toward her. It was lucky they'd gone over the rules, because here was the test run, and Steven bent and pecked her rosy cheek, wrapping an arm around her waist.

"Gin, this is Cassidy." He watched the lights turn on in Ginny's eyes, and he prayed she kept her cool. "She's a family friend," he continued, surprising himself with how true the description rang.

Cassidy stuck her hand out to shake. "Hi. Sorry… What's your name?"

"Ginny."

"Nice to meet you." They dropped hands. "Has Steven told you about Thanksgiving?"

Ginny checked with him quickly before answering. "Yeah... I mean, yes. He said you... Well, your families have a tradition."

"My mom is a big Thanksgiving person. She invites everyone and anyone." Cassidy hitched her hip and jammed a hand into her back pocket, her stance so comfortable and casual Steven had almost forgotten what that looked like. Ginny only got that relaxed after a good hour in his presence.

"One year she asked us to invite the mail lady because she looked sad," Steven said with a laugh. "Cass and I had to chase her down to give her the invite."

The corner of Ginny's mouth lifted, and a sad sparkle settled in her eyes. She shifted Cocoa into one arm, and then tentatively slid her hand around Steven's waist. A shock reverberated through his chest, and he suppressed a shiver running up his spine.

"That's sweet." Ginny said. The side of their hips pressed together, their arms wrapped like they were... like they were a couple. Steven could almost convince himself that they were.

"And crazy," Cassidy joked, pulling him out of the bubble he was setting up around him and Ginny. "Anyway, Steven said you were a fantastic baker."

Ginny jerked in his arm, and he gave her a sheepish grin. "He... He did?"

Cassidy laughed. "He was totally bragging about you. I

hoped you'd save us all and take care of the pies for Thanksgiving. My mom would like to think she's got a handle on it, but she really... I mean *really* doesn't."

"I... Well, I... Um..." She shot a petrified stare at him, and a wave of embarrassment ran through his neck. He probably should've brought this up earlier, and he might have if he'd remembered.

"There's no pressure," Cassidy quickly added. She flicked her eyes to Steven, understanding settling in her dark chocolate irises. "Let me know?"

Steven nodded, and Cassidy let out a long sigh. "Well, I better jet." She gave Ginny another smile. "It was great meeting you. See you next week."

Was Thanksgiving really that soon? His hand twitched against Ginny's hip, almost as if he knew just how close she was to no longer being his girlfriend.

Or fake girlfriend.

Cassidy went back into the shelter, and Ginny slowly dropped her arm from his waist. His body felt suddenly empty.

"So..." she said, raising her brow. "I'm a fantastic baker?"

fourteen

Ginny's laptop sat on the coffee table in the living room, a half a dozen tabs open in her internet. There were about fifteen thousand sites on emotional support animals, and the crushing, overwhelming anxiety of getting all the information she could before asking the landlord was enough to put Ginny out of commission for a week.

She clicked over to her resume, checking it *again* for typos. The deadline to apply was closing in, and she was pretty sure she wasn't the gung-ho confident woman she'd wanted to be after a week with Steven, but she felt good enough to at least apply. The interview on the other hand was another story, and she'd cross that bridge when she came to it—after losing a lot of sleep over it, of course.

The front door opened, and her heart pitter-pattered to an up-tempo number. Lauren let out an exhausted sigh, putting her keys onto the hook and placing her purse on the side table. She bent, tucking her forefinger into her shoe and tugging it off. It hit the rug with a thud.

"Long… Long day?" Ginny said, her voice shaky all because of what she needed to ask Lauren. If Lauren was already in a mood, this might not go over well, but Ginny didn't want to wait much longer to run the adoption idea by her. Cocoa was such a sweetie; she imagined every second she waited was another second someone else could adopt her.

"We rearranged the self-help sections today," she said, slumping into the couch and tossing an arm over her eyes. "You know how many books the library has on weight loss?"

"A thousand?"

Lauren pursed her lips, keeping her laughter at bay. "Sure felt like it."

"Maybe one of those can be our next book club book," Ginny tried to joke.

"A diet book for December? I doubt any of us wants guilt for Christmas."

They shared a small laugh, and Ginny dropped her gaze to the quilt over her legs. She played with the ties, her thoughts drifting to the other day in her bed when Steven had given Ginny her first kiss. He hadn't said anything about it, not that she expected him to, but she wondered if he knew just how special it'd been for her. Even if it wasn't real for him, it was very real for her.

"Um… Can I talk to you about something?" she asked, keeping her fingers twined in the yarn. Lauren lifted her head and straightened in the couch.

"Are you okay?"

She nodded… then started to shake her head with a laugh. "Just nervous."

"I'm not that scary, am I?" Lauren said, the corner of her mouth turning up. Ginny tried to smile, but she ended up blowing out a shaky breath instead.

"Now you have me nervous." Lauren adjusted on the couch, tucking her feet under her and pushing her long hair behind her ear. "Is… is it Steven?"

Ginny's eyes widened. "Wha… No, no. Things are going… really well with him." She took a deep breath and reached for her laptop. She clicked onto the shelter's site and slid the screen around so Lauren could see. "I was thinking… of adopting her."

Her words floated through the air while Lauren silently considered. Ginny didn't feel right asking the landlord before asking Lauren, considering Lauren was covering part of her rent.

"Are you moving out?" Lauren asked, her voice hitching. "You have a year lease."

"I don't want to move out, no."

Lauren's brows pinched in concern. "Ginny, you know we can't have pets."

"Yes. But… Well, I was thinking… Maybe there'd be an exception?"

"What kind of exception?"

Ginny clicked to the page on emotional support animals and lease rules for Washington State. She took in a shaky breath and tried to explain without losing her nerve.

"I've met her a few times," she said. "Cocoa… the doggy… and she's been good for me. And I can train her to come around with me everywhere, so there wouldn't be any worry over leaving her here alone, and Steven is across the street, too. He's really good with animals; I'm sure he'd help. And whatever damage she does, I'll pay for. I'll make sure we get the deposit back when we move out. I just... I thought there was no harm in asking."

Sadness flashed in Lauren's light brown eyes. She smoothed her hands down her bright blue high waisted skirt, and Ginny waited with bated breath for her to collect her thoughts. If she had to say no—which was entirely possible—it was going to take her a while. Lauren hated telling people what they didn't want to hear.

"I think we should run it by the other girls," she said after a moment. Ginny's stomach leapt.

"You... You're not saying no?"

Lauren chuckled. "I think an emotional support animal is a great idea for you, but we have to make sure it's okay with everybody. And then you can ask the landlord."

Hope bubbled under Ginny's skin. "Can we... can we do that now?" She didn't want to wait a second longer. She'd call the landlord that evening if she got the thumbs up from everyone living there.

Lauren pushed out of the couch. "I'll see if Marcy and April are home if you want to get Ashlynn."

Ginny practically bounced down the hallway and rapped on Ashlynn's door. Ashlynn answered in a cute dress, her hair half-curled and her face makeup ready. She must have a date tonight, unsurprisingly.

"Um... you got a minute?" Ginny asked, and Ashlynn followed her into the living room where they waited for everyone else.

Ten minutes later, all five girls raised their hands, voting Cocoa into the house. Ginny was on the phone with the landlord before they'd all retreated back to their own rooms.

She stepped out onto the porch to get some quiet while she explained—with quite the conviction—the situation to the landlord, a sweet older man who'd rented out about twenty or so locations to college students. Her eyes caught Batman and Robin playing happily in the Atkinson's front yard, and she squinted to the porch, hoping to see Steven sitting there.

"It's a small dog, right?" her landlord confirmed.

"A Pomeranian mix, I think," she answered, smiling when she saw Steven shift into view on his porch. "She's full grown. I could fit her in a grocery bag."

Hope kindled in her heart; he wasn't outright saying no. He was either cruel or seriously considering it.

"Tell you what, Miss Thompkins. I'll make this one time exception if you promise not to spread the word around that I'm a softy."

She blinked. "You're... you're saying it's okay?"

"I'll be out there during Thanksgiving weekend to update the stove—gonna hit those Black Friday sales—and I'll check in and make sure the dog is a good idea. If it's not, then you'll have to find a new place to live when your lease is up."

"Okay, okay. Thank you. Thank you so much."

"Have a good holiday."

"You too." She hung up, her hands shaking with utter disbelief. Cocoa was hers as soon as she got her butt down to the shelter. She didn't think it was possible. There were rules. Strict ones. And she never would've even thought to ask or had the guts to if it hadn't been for the guy across the street.

She pounced off the porch steps, barely looking both ways before crossing the road. As much as she loved those Labrador puppies, she paid them no attention and darted right for Steven.

He was playing with his phone, leaning his elbows on his knees, but straightened when she climbed his porch steps. His dimples appeared, deep and happy.

"Hey," he said.

"Hi."

She nibbled her lip briefly, but her excitement would not relent. Her feet scaled the porch, and she sat sideways on his lap, wrapping her arms around his neck. A sharp breath of surprise zipped past his lips, buzzing in her ear, and she held on, trying not to analyze her spontaneity.

"I can get Cocoa," she said, squeezing him tighter. One of his big hands rested on her thigh while the other gripped her hip and hitched her up on his lap.

"W-what?" he croaked, suddenly seeming more nervous than her, which she never thought possible. She laughed, leaning back to meet his eyes.

"Cocoa. My landlord said I could adopt her."

He blinked, his soul smiling behind those baby blues. Batman and Robin's nails scraped against the wood of the porch, and a cold nose pushed against Ginny's ankles.

"Wait, you can take her?"

She nodded, her smile unable to fade. "Can we go now? She's still there, right? I can bring her home today?"

Her body shifted with his laughter. "Hell yeah. Let me get Jemma to watch these little devils."

"I got you, bro!" They heard from inside the screen door. Warmth smacked her cheeks at being caught sitting so comfortably on Steven's lap. Why was it so comfortable? She didn't even move when Jemma opened the door and stepped onto the porch.

"Come on, superheroes," Jemma said to the puppies, patting her leg. "Your dad has to spend time with his girl."

As red as she was, Ginny liked the sound of being Steven's girl. Maybe she ought to embrace it while she could. After Thanksgiving, she'd be back to being no one's girl.

Jemma went inside with the labs, and Steven rolled his eyes to Ginny. "Sorry. She gets all too excited at the idea of me dating."

Ginny tucked her hair behind her ear, her fingers lingering in the blue ends, twisting and twirling the strands. If she was honest, she was excited about the idea as well, even if it was all for show.

She slowly rose from his lap, already missing the comfort of his hand on her leg, his grip on her hip. But Cocoa was waiting, and she didn't want that poor pup trapped in a kennel any longer.

Steven must've sensed her urgency, because he took her hand. "Meet me by Grandpa's car. I'll grab the keys."

Using her excitement for fuel, she pushed up on her toes and pressed a kiss to his cheek, then bounced off the porch and practically danced her way to the silver Cadillac. It wasn't until she leaned against the passenger side door that she noticed Steven still standing on the porch, watching her dork out with an amused grin. As their eyes locked, he shook his head, then ducked inside. Ginny touched her tingling lips, hoping that she'd find the guts to kiss his cheek again before she just became another girl to him.

fifteen

Tonight a good night for pie?

His text shot off with a whoosh, and Steven sat back and played with his phone while he waited for it to vibrate. Jemma and Grandpa were getting ready for their date night, and he was itching to see Ginny again without an audience. They hadn't been truly alone since last Sunday in her bed.

Was it insane that his lips missed hers? It'd been the shortest kiss he'd probably ever given anyone, lingering for only a moment before he'd pulled away, unwilling to push it. As first kisses go, it'd rocked his entire world off axis. He couldn't remember the last time that'd happened. Not since Cassidy, he knew that much for certain.

All he could hope was that he wasn't ruining things. He could see her confidence growing, a light that she'd always had in her coming out for everyone else to enjoy, too. A pang of guilt dug in his gut that he hadn't really helped her in applying for that job she wanted. Every time they were together, his mind was so distracted he forgot a whole lot of things. Like the fact that she wasn't his real girlfriend.

His phone buzzed, and he fumbled to open it, laughing at himself for being so ridiculous. It was a selfie of her in the kitchen, a cookbook sitting open on the counter next to a bunch of ingredients.

Good timing, the caption read. He grinned and leapt from the couch, Batman and Robin both perking their heads up with his sudden movement. He let out a sigh, frowning at the pups. He'd neglected them enough that week.

Can I bring the demon pups? They can hang out outside.

The bubbles popped up right away, so he sat and waited for the response.

Yes! I want Cocoa to have more interactions with dogs. She's attached to my hip!

He chuckled, heading for the leashes hanging on the wall by the door. The labs pounced to his feet and jumped up his legs.

Who could blame her? ;)

He sent that off and tucked his phone away, imagining her blush at the compliment as he clicked his pups up and let them drag him across the street. It was getting dark, the clouds looking ominously gray overhead. They'd had rain here and there that week, but it wasn't too cold yet. It was the first night he felt he really needed to swap his hoodie out for a thicker coat.

He hurried up the porch steps and pushed the doorbell. "Knock it off," he scolded Batman, who was scratching at the screen door. When the lock clicked, he tightened his grip on the leashes, knowing his dogs were going to go wild when they saw Cocoa. And Ginny, for that matter. She was pretty much their favorite person.

Her honey eyes peeked out from the crack in the door, and she gave him a smile. "You… mind if we take this slow?" she asked. "I'm not sure how Cocoa Puff will react.

How was she… you know… with the other dogs at the shelter?"

He bobbed his head back and forth. "She was good with 'em, but I'm not sure how different it'll be now that she's with you."

"What do you mean?"

"Well, she's happy now." He watched Ginny's eyes light up and her cheeks turn a shade of dusty rose. "So she might be a little protective of you."

Ginny pulled the door open wider inch by inch. The fuzzy brown dog peeked out, and the second she saw Steven, she buried her face into Ginny's neck and whimpered.

"It's just Steven," Ginny consoled the scared pup. "You like him, don't you?"

"She probably associates me with the shelter," he said, easing the screen door open. "You mind if I let these guys run in the backyard, and she can join them when she's ready?"

"That's a good idea." Ginny moved back, waving toward the kitchen. "Right through there. Probably where yours is."

He padded across the rug in the living room, his dogs wrestling one another and tripping him up the whole way into the backyard. Ginny's house had a smaller backyard than Grandpa's but still plenty of room for them to run around. He slid the door shut behind him and let them loose. Robin found the first tree and lifted his leg while Batman sniffed a bit before marking his spots.

The sliding glass door opened with a swoosh, and

Ginny stepped outside, Cocoa in one arm and a big bowl of water in the other. She set the bowl down at the bottom of the steps and offered Steven a grin. There was something different about her, too, but he couldn't quite put his finger on it.

"Will that be enough?" she asked, gesturing to the water. He was touched she thought to give them a drink at all.

"I'll refill it if they go through it all," he said, closing the distance between them. His gaze fell to the little bear pup in her arms, and he tentatively reached out to scratch Cocoa's ears.

"Hey, girl," he said. The dog stuffed her face back into Ginny's neck, and Ginny let out a little giggle that set Steven's chest on fire.

"You see what I mean about attached?"

He smirked, stroking the pup's soft fur. "How's she doing otherwise? Any signs of aggression? What about accidents in the house? She eating enough?"

Ginny pursed her lips together, amusement sparkling in her eyes.

"What?" he asked.

"It's... cute... You worrying about her."

He rolled his eyes, but the compliment burrowed into his chest and lit him up. "Not just her," he clarified. "I worry about you, too."

Ginny adjusted Cocoa in her arms, coaxing the dog out from hiding. Cocoa sniffed Steven's hand for a bit before giving him a sloppy kiss across the knuckles.

"Yes on eating enough," Ginny finally answered, maneuvering around him and heading inside. Steven made sure the demon pups were behaving themselves, then followed. Ginny bent, setting Cocoa on the laminate kitchen floor. His gaze locked on her curves, how her pants hugged her legs and butt perfectly, and that tiny strip of skin peeking out between her shirt and waistband. He swallowed hard and blinked. It took a full five seconds for him to snap out of it.

"Uh… What about aggression?" he asked, running a hand over the back of his neck. Was it hot in here? He'd better take his jacket off.

Ginny shook her head. "She's still the sweetest dog. Just a little shy."

"Understatement," he joked, eyeing Cocoa nuzzled up to Ginny's legs. The dog wouldn't dare go near him. He'd be offended if he wasn't so amused by the bond she already had with her owner.

Ginny leaned on the counter, tucking her chin in her hand as she stared at the open cookbook. An overwhelmed sigh filled the room. She was the most adorable thing he'd ever seen, and he sidled up next to her, resting a hand on the counter to read over her shoulder.

"Which one are we starting with?"

"I don't think it matters," she said, flipping the pages between pumpkin and banana cream pie. "I will mess up either one."

"Such little faith."

She lifted her gaze to his. "You know those cookies I made? That was some of my best work in the kitchen."

He pushed the page open to pumpkin and smoothed it out. "If all else fails, we go store bought and put it in a home dish."

"You're buying," she said, straightening. "It's your fault we're in this mess, after all."

He laughed, mesmerized by her as she crossed the kitchen and reached up for a mixing bowl. There was that strip of skin again. Her hair was so long that the turquoise ends brushed along the small of her back. Her fingers tripped over the smooth surface of the bowl, trying to get a good grip on it to bring it down.

"Um... a little help?" she teased him, breaking him from his ogling. He jumped to her rescue, pulling the bowl from the shelf and setting it next to the pumpkin spice. Cocoa perched between Ginny's legs, and that's when it hit him.

Ginny was different... still her, but more sure of herself. She hadn't stuttered through her thoughts, and she teased him without abandon. He knew that she'd be good for that dog, but he had no idea how good that dog would be for her.

"Okay," she said with a heavy sigh, her hands fumbling with a pie tin. "Cross your fingers I don't botch this."

sixteen

The oven door creaked as Ginny pulled it open and slid the pie inside. It smelled good, at least. It wasn't the best looking thing on the planet, but she planned to cover that up with lots of whipped cream.

Cocoa scurried between her legs, and Ginny shut the oven and set the timer. She was not going to be distracted by Steven this time, no matter how easy it was.

"Are there any other talents you bragged about that I don't possess?" she asked, crossing her arms and playfully hitching her hip. She had no idea who this person was right now—this Ginny who spoke without umming or pausing every few seconds. But she liked her; she could get used to having her around.

Steven pushed his hair back, leaving a streak of flour in the pitch black strands. "Thinking…" he said with a tap to his chin. She took a deep breath for courage, using Cocoa's warm fur to keep her calm before she strode over and wiped the flour out of his hair.

A buzz ran under her skin at the softness of the strands, and she tried not to get distracted by the light in his eyes.

"Damn…" he whispered under his breath. She pinched her brows together.

"What?"

He shook his head. "You're just..." He lifted a shoulder. "Different tonight. Not a bad different, but..."

Her teeth grabbed hold of the inside of her lip, and she only chewed once before giving him a grin. "I feel different." She knocked into his shoulder. "Not a bad different."

"Think you can take on that job now?" he asked, crossing his arms and leaning against the counter. His eyes briefly strayed to the window before returning to hers.

"If I can have Cocoa in there with me." She playfully wriggled the dog sitting between her ankles. "Or you, for that matter."

Confusion tugged at his expression, and a slab of rock plummeted into the pit of her stomach. She wanted to suck those words right back inside her mouth, but her inhibitions had taken advantage, and now one of her secret thoughts was out there.

When silence crept over them, he nudged her with his elbow. "What do you mean by that, Gin?"

"Oh... I... Well... Cocoa is my emotional support animal."

"Yeah..." He rotated his hand around, urging her to elaborate. She decided playing dumb was a lot safer.

"So I'd be more confident with her around."

He rotated his hand again. Of course he wasn't satisfied with that half answer, but she wasn't going to admit she considered him to also be an emotional support. That would put a thousand pounds of pressure on him, and they were, after all, only in this together until Thanksgiving.

She picked up a toy cornucopia and fiddled with the

plastic gourd hanging out of it. "We should... Well... we should probably go over a few things before the dinner next week, right?" Great, she was back to stuttering. Not just her words, but her heart, her nerves. She pushed back a piece of hair that had fallen out of her ponytail and looked out the window. "A practice run, maybe? How intrusive is Cassidy's family?"

Steven snorted, snatching the cornucopia from her hands. "Expect a lot of embarrassing stories about me, about her, about us together."

"Even... I mean... I'll be there. So..."

"Yeah, having significant others around won't stop Cass's mom from hitting the bottle too hard and running her mouth."

Ginny bit her lip. "What about Jemma? She'll be there, too, right?"

"Mmmhmm."

"And Grandpa?"

"Yep."

"And..." She gulped, gazing down at her new doggie. "Can I bring Cocoa?"

His lip perked up in the corner, his dimple looking extra deep with the pitiful lighting in the clubhouse kitchen. "I don't see that being a problem."

She let out a sigh of relief. "Okay. I-I think I can handle a drunk mom conversation."

He set the cornucopia down, and his hand smoothed across her back and rested on her waist. A spike of energy ran through her suddenly warm veins, and she shivered slightly.

"You'll be great, Gin." He leaned down, knocking foreheads with her. Her body was on an electric wire, pinging and zapping and wishing he'd close the gap between their mouths once more. Cocoa stirred against her leg, but no comforting furry animal could quell the storm rising within her.

"Thank you for doing this for me," he said, and as suddenly as he was in her space, he was gone. A sad smile touched his lips, and he stared out the window. "I keep thinking that if I get through this dinner, maybe I can come clean with Cass. Tell her everything. But... guess I'm just not ready for that yet."

Like the moon can eclipse the sun, Ginny's buzz darkened. She subtly slid down the counter, putting some distance between them so she wasn't acutely aware of his skin every time it brushed against hers.

"You're... um... you're welcome." She winced at the crack in her voice. She quickly picked up Cocoa, not only for comfort but for something to do with her hands. There weren't going to be any more brushes through his hair or arms around waists. She couldn't take the sudden reminders that Steven was in love with someone else, and she was there to get him through the holiday.

"Hey," he said, breaking her from her sad thoughts. He pointed out the window and pushed from the counter. "I think it's snowing."

"What?"

"Yeah." His grin widened, and he headed for the sliding

glass door, peering out into the backyard. "Come on."

He held his hand out for hers, but she—as politely as she could—slipped past it, clinging to Cocoa as she stepped into the chilly night air.

Wet dots covered the concrete, but nothing was sticking yet. Ginny cast her eyes upward, waiting for the first sign of winter.

Steven stepped behind her, his warmth frustratingly comforting. She shrank into it, and his arms wrapped around her and Cocoa.

Don't you go falling for him, she warned her beating heart.

He rocked her in the sweet silence, and she closed her eyes, pretending like he wasn't going to disappear from her life in a week. He wanted to tell Cassidy everything—did that mean he'd include the fake relationship he'd had with Ginny?

"Hey," he said, whispering in her ear. "Do you see it?"

Her eyes fluttered open and followed his finger to a single snowflake drifting from the black sky.

"Yay," she squeaked softly, pushing her face into the fur of her pup. "First snowfall of the season."

"Grandpa'll be building his snow fort any day now," he said with a laugh, his deep voice vibrating through his chest and against her back.

"I want to help," she said, testing the waters of where they'd be when snow covered the ground.

"Don't tell him that," Steven said. "He'll be knocking down your door after every major snow fall."

"That'd... I mean... I'd be okay with that."

His hand twitched against her, and he slowly spun her around, his brows pulled in concern when their eyes met. "Are you okay?"

"Yes." She checked her answer and decided on something a bit more honest. "Kinda."

He smirked. "Thought so. What's going on? Did I do something?" His eyes fell to her waist. "Am I okay to hug you like this?"

She wanted to know what it meant to him. For her, showing any physical affection was deeply meaningful, but probably because it took so much courage for her to accept and give it. But she knew it wasn't like that for everyone, especially people like Steven. He was naturally bold and didn't overthink every time he touched someone.

Her fingers squeezed Cocoa, and the dog complied, snuggling into her neck and providing the strength Ginny needed. She wasn't going to admit so much—not now when there was just a week until Thanksgiving. She wasn't going to ruin their deal, especially since he'd done so much for her confidence already.

"Yes," she said. "We're friends, right?"

He raised a brow. "I hope so."

"Friends hug."

The corners of his mouth tugged downward. "Yeah… But…"

"But?"

He smiled, reaching for Cocoa and giving her a good pat. "Just wondering what's going through your head. You're always so quiet."

She was, and she knew it, but she was quiet for good reason. So she simply lifted a shoulder, and he let out a frustrated, playful grunt, spinning her back around and holding her again. Cocoa poked her head out from Ginny's neck and sniffed at Steven's collar, and Ginny really couldn't blame her. He smelled like pumpkin dessert.

The snow slowly picked up, and Batman and Robin perked their ears, snouts raised to the sky at the phenomenon.

"Is this their first time seeing snow?" Ginny asked, excitement bubbling through her.

"Sure is." Steven's arms dropped from her waist, and he crouched down. Robin scurried over to Steven and pushed his head under Steven's arm. Batman was out chasing each flake as it fell, biting at the air.

"They're like me and you," Ginny said with a laugh, gesturing to the two puppies. "I hide from all these new things, and you just go for it."

"Or I drag you into the fun," he said as Batman pounced over to his brother, barking and wagging his tail. After a good minute, Robin eased out from under Steven's protection and followed Batman into the yard. Within minutes they were snow-covered from head to toe.

Steven scooped up a handful and patted it into a ball. "You having any buyer's remorse?" he asked, nodding to Cocoa in her arms.

Ginny braced herself in case he decided to send that snowball her direction. Her shoulders slipped into a casual stance the second he lobbed it up in the air and the two labs fought for custody.

"Not one bit." She snuggled the pup before setting her gently on the snow-covered grass. Cocoa wasn't going to go out and play—Ginny was well aware—but she did lick the air every time a snowflake got close. "I think she knows I need her," Ginny said, not really meaning for Steven to hear. It was more of her thinking out loud.

She tentatively looked his way, and he was unexpectedly close. The dimple in his left cheek indented, while his right cheek was smoother. His eyes held hers with mesmerizing strength. She really wished he'd stop doing that; she had enough trouble controlling her thoughts without him giving her these adorable, intense gazes with those ocean blues.

"Or maybe," he said, stepping into her. "Maybe she needed you."

Her breath was lost to the sky, and somewhere her brain registered Cocoa rubbing against her shin. Was he getting even closer? Was that his eyes dropping to her lips? Panic rushed through her chest, and her heart stopped beating for a full second. He couldn't kiss her, because what would that mean? It couldn't be for practice, could it? And friends certainly did not kiss. If they did, she wouldn't have had virgin lips for twenty-two years.

His brows pulled in, and he kinked his neck to the side. She wondered what sort of expression she was wearing to make him suddenly stop. Probably a human version of a scared kitty cat.

"Gin?" he asked. "Do you... smell something?"

Her brain skipped over to his train of thinking like

conversational whiplash. It took her at least five seconds to sniff the air a few times and five more for her stomach to drop.

"Oh no..." She whipped to the house. "The pie!"

Through the sliding glass door, smoke billowed from the oven, filling up the kitchen. The smoke detector cut through the air, and Steven rushed inside, calling over his shoulder, "Stay outside with the dogs!"

Ginny hurried for the pups, snatching Batman and Robin's collars before they could follow Steven. She led them through the gate and around front, grateful that Cocoa was already a good follower and praying that Steven either knew how to stop a smoking pie or had the smarts to get the heck out of there before the whole house went down.

So much for that deposit.

seventeen

"Stop laughing at me!" Ginny covered her face with her hands. Steven continued to chuckle, pulling at her arms.

"I'm not laughing at you," he assured her. "Just... the situation."

"The situation?" She gawked at him, then swung her hand around at the neighborhood all standing outside taking pictures of the firemen. Channel 5 was there, interviewing Steven's very enthusiastic grandpa who was in nothing but his boxers.

"There I was, doing my yoga for the night, and I see little Ginny and my grandson's dogs rushing out in the middle of the road. Well, that's when the smoke alarms started blazing—I swear to it, they could be heard in China—and I called the fire brigade, picked up my extinguisher, and went right over in my skivvies. Good thing, too, 'cause bless my grandson's heart, he don't know what the hell he's doing when it comes to putting out a good ol' fashioned cooking fire."

Steven pointed over at his grandpa. "See? He's throwing me under the bus, not you. Nothing to worry about."

"The whole neighborhood is out here." Her eyes grew wider and wider. "And what about my landlord? Oh goodness, I just convinced him to bend the rules for me, and I burn down the house!"

Steven suppressed another laugh, tucking her under his arm and pulling her against his chest. "You didn't burn anything. Except a pie."

She mumbled something into his jacket he didn't catch, but she was so darn cute so frustrated like this, he couldn't help his amusement.

His phone vibrated in his pocket, and he adjusted Ginny so he could see who it was.

Grandpa is on the news! Is everything okay???

Cassidy. He swiped across his keyboard, chuckling as he typed.

Little accident with the practice pies Ginny was making. We're all good, but prepare for store bought dessert.

Ginny shifted in his arms, and he clicked his phone off and tucked it away. Her embarrassment had faded, but her frown was still in place.

"You okay?" he asked, running a finger over the wrinkle in her forehead. She gently moved away from his touch.

"Um... Was that... I mean, I wasn't trying to read your messages, but... Am I fired from making dessert?"

"I wouldn't say that." He already missed having her against him, but she didn't exactly look like she wanted to be held anymore, her arms crossed and ice in her honey eyes. "I'd say you're off the hook."

Her lips pursed, and she gave him one short nod. "Okay."

"Hey," he said, reaching for her but pulling back when she brushed him off. "I'm sorry if I offended you with that text. I was joking."

"I... I know."

She blew out a breath of smoke into the cold air, her eyes cutting to something just over his shoulder. Relief colored her cheeks. "I'm going to... Well, Lauren just got here. So I'd better..."

"Oh right. Yeah." He stepped aside, letting her take the widest berth possible around him to talk to her stunned roommate. His brows pinched together, and he yanked his phone back out, analyzing every word he'd sent to Cassidy. Maybe he should've clarified that it was both of them who'd let that pie burn. Honestly, he'd been so enamored with Ginny out in the first drops of snow the whole house could've blown up without him noticing.

He lifted his gaze. Ginny's arms were bare, and he unzipped his jacket, beating himself up for not offering it to her sooner. His phone buzzed again, and he sighed at the text.

LOL. Anything is better than Mom's. I'm not worried. Tell Ginny no pressure. Also, so glad everyone is okay. Tell Grandpa he's lookin' good ;)

The corner of his mouth picked up. *Will do.*

A thunk hit the side of his head, and he spun around, rubbing the spot.

"What was that for?" he asked his sister. Jemma hitched a hand up on her hip and shook her head.

"Gosh, you're so stupid." She nodded toward Ginny.

"You have any idea how lucky you are a girl like that even gives you the time of day?"

"Yeah," he said, his jaw clenching. "I do."

"Then why the hell are you talking to the ex?"

He stuffed his phone into his pocket and swung his jacket over his arm. He didn't owe Jemma any explanation.

"Cass and I are friends."

"Uh huh."

"She's got a boyfriend, Jemma."

"And you've got a girlfriend."

He wished. But it wasn't fair to pursue Ginny right now. Not when he was still confused, and especially not when he'd asked her to fake their relationship. He wasn't sure she even thought of him in that way.

He bit his tongue and turned away from his sister. She'd only yell at him for playing around with Ginny. He deserved it, but that didn't mean he wanted to hear it.

Jemma let out an exasperated sigh. "Look, all I'm saying, from a female perspective, no girl likes the feeling of second best. So when Ginny's freaking out about something—like, I don't know, the fire department showing up at her house—then maybe you should be giving her all your attention and not divvying it out between her and Cassidy."

Hell, he had done that. She was in his arms when he responded. Maybe it wasn't so much the words at all but responding. Would that have bothered her? They weren't technically dating, but sometimes it felt that way. Sometimes it felt so easy to take her hand, hold her, lean down to kiss her. Harsh reminders that she wasn't actually his hurt more than he'd expected.

He watched Ginny across the street, red lights flashing across her face from the fire engine. A rush of energy zapped through him, and the fear of losing her gripped his heart. Could he be falling for her while still in love with someone else?

He swallowed hard and dropped his gaze to the jacket in his hands. "Will you give this to her?" he asked Jemma. "She's probably freezing."

He stuffed his hands in his pockets and headed home to be alone with his dogs and his thoughts.

eighteen

Ginny stepped into work the next day, her spine a little straighter and a bounce in her step. After the terrifying prospect that she'd be kicked out of her place, she was grateful that her landlord was an understanding person. Perhaps too understanding; he actually took most of the blame. The oven was supposed to be replaced two weeks ago, but he'd put it off till after Thanksgiving. Even though it wasn't his fault in the slightest, Ginny let herself feel relief and absolved herself of the guilt that had eaten at her all night.

She also had a good talk with herself—and Cocoa—about Steven. There had been too many reminders last night that he still loved his ex, and she replayed them in her head to keep her heart on track. This was not a mission to fall in love but to get a job. With her resume ready to go, she was going to hit that send button.

As usual, Alex didn't stroll into work until about ten, but she wasn't going to let that bug her today. He was her test subject, and she was going to try a little of that confidence she'd gained.

"Morning," she said without a hitch in her voice. She even put on a smile. He blinked and paused for a second before giving her a return grin and head nod.

"Mornin', Gin Rummy. Gorgeous day, wouldn't you say?"

Oh good, he was in a fun mood. That would help her, she hoped. It was still intimidating, but not as scary as trying to converse with a grump.

"A little cloudy," she said with a laugh. "The snow's gone, though."

"Damn shame, if you ask me." He slid an earbud into his ear. He picked up some of the heavier packages and loaded them onto the cart.

"You... you like the snow?" Shoot, she'd tripped up on that one. She closed her eyes and refocused. It was easier with Steven; she wasn't terrified of him judging her or taking things the wrong way. He made her nervous and comfortable all at the same time and in the best way possible.

"More like what happens when it snows," he said with a wink. She tilted her head to the side.

"What do you mean?"

He made a sex motion with his fist, and let out a bolt of laughter when her eyes nearly bulged from her head. "It's an aphrodisiac. First snow of the season? Romantic as hell."

Sure... She supposed she could see that. Before the fire trucks last night, it'd been extremely romantic. When Steven wrapped his hand around her sleeve and pulled her close, a shot of heat had run through her. It wasn't... bad. It was ice cream in summer, a blanket in winter. It was hot chocolate on the porch with a good book. It was new shoes, fuzzy socks, cuddling with puppies.

It was pure comfort, and Ginny had no idea that sort of thing existed within a single person.

She blinked back into the present and put on a teasing smile. "But, isn't every night like that for you, pretty much?"

"Damn, Rummy. Was that a dig?"

"Maybe." Her heart beat double time, but it wasn't in a bad way. She liked being this person—fun and teasing. Alex even seemed impressed.

He lifted another box and slammed it onto the cart. "Well, last night was special."

"You got away without learning her name?" she quipped. Look at her go. She was joking around... about *sex*. Pride lifted in her chest, but it didn't hang around. Alex's jaw clenched, his eyes narrowing. The joking air around them disappeared with one blink of his cold eyes. Ginny's pride tipped over from the blow, landing somewhere outside of her.

"I'm... I'm sorry," she whispered, her gaze darting to the mail she was sorting. She didn't dare look his way, fear eating at the backs of her eyeballs and tangling her tongue.

"This one is special, Gin. So it's not a joke, all right?"

She nodded, her fingers fumbling over the letters, embarrassment blurring her vision. Another apology sat on her tongue, but her voice had been locked away in a cage, and over the course of one conversation, all her confidence wisped into the air like it'd never been there in the first place.

She moved to the side as he pushed the mail cart past, his grip tight on the handlebar, his forearm muscle bulging the teddy bear ninja tattoo. Ginny's breath didn't return until the distinct bell of the elevator rang through the mail room.

She pressed the heels of her hands into her eyes, shoving back the oncoming tears she did not want to release. What had she done? Had she just ruined the relationship with the only coworker she talked to in a matter of seconds? She needed Cocoa. She needed something to snuggle into, to soak up this clawing feeling in her chest, this panic that gripped her throat and dug its nails into her skull. Guilt crashed down on her, and she crumpled to the floor, knocking off a stack of letters.

How did one breathe again? Her body wasn't cooperating, and her mind was in constant replay of what her mouth had done. She could only imagine speaking in confidence with clients or potential clients, and that was even if she got past the interview stage. Why had she sent off that resume? She should've tested herself out first. She wasn't ready for this.

Her fingers dug into her chest, and she forced herself to breathe. *In... out... in... out...* The bike tattoo on her wrist had faded to almost nothing, and she studied the lines sinking into her skin.

She ran a thumb over the ink, zoning into a memory of not long ago when Steven had done the same thing.

One stray tear fell from her lashes and rolled down her cheek. Her fingers trembled near her hip while she contemplated calling him. That comfort he gave her had never gone away, even with the fact that he was in love with someone else. A friend could be just as good, if not better, than a lover in these sorts of circumstances. She only wanted a hand to hold—a direct line of courage.

After sucking in a large breath, she pulled her phone out and dialed. It rang three times, and after each ring she nearly hung up.

"Hey," his warm and friendly voice greeted, and that alone relaxed her heart. "I was just thinking about you. What's up?"

She nibbled on her lip and eyed her wrist. "Are you… Are you busy after work today?"

He paused for a beat, long enough for her to think that he did have plans and didn't want to say no to her. But then his voice came back, and she envisioned that dimpled smile in his response. "Not really. What do you want to do?"

She wiped the tear from her face and stared at the mail surrounding her. There was no future for her there. It wasn't what she longed to do with her career, and if she was ever going to get her butt out of the mailroom and into a therapist chair, then she had to find that courage somewhere deep within her and overcome this fear of everything.

"Meet me at the address I'm going to text you? I… I think I'm ready to finally do something I've always wanted to do."

nineteen

It took Steven an hour just to get through traffic. His grandpa's Cadillac wasn't up for the job, either, popping and pinging the whole way. And forget the heater. If Steven wanted to warm up he was going to have to bury himself into the black and blue hoodie he'd thrown on last second.

The address Ginny had sent was a little out of their neck of the woods, and he wondered if she'd taken an Uber or something to get there. He could offer her a ride home—if she didn't mind sitting in an icebox. At least he'd have the chance to make up for not offering his jacket to her the night of the burnt pie.

He pulled up a little ways from his destination, snagging the only available parking space he could see on the road. The parking meter accepted cards, so he swiped for an hour and headed up the street.

He spotted her up the sidewalk, pulling on the sleeves of a bright pink sweater. She brought her hands up, blowing warm breath against her fingers. Her ear-flapped hat hung loosely over her hair, which blew softly in the wind. If he'd been just passing by, he imagined pausing for a second, third, and fourth look, just to see if someone as gorgeous as her actually existed.

His pace quickened against the rain-slicked concrete,

deeper puddles splashing up his jeans. The snow had melted over the weekend, and there hadn't been another sign of it since. But the leaves were still falling and littering the streets, autumn refusing to give in to winter.

The street lights flickered on, and he squinted at the building behind Ginny. A graffiti-ed sign that read Tommy's Tats lit up the turquoise in her hair.

Steven slid his hands into his pockets, an grin forming on his lips as he stepped up to her. "Conquering that fear of needles?" he asked. She spun around, a sparkle twinkling in her eyes before a smile dropped to her lips.

"Hi," she said.

"Hey."

She pulled on her hat flaps, twisting the braided strings that hung from each ear. "Thanks for coming."

"No problem." He gazed up at the tattoo parlor's sign. "What exactly are we doing?"

"Right now?" She blew out a breath. "Trying to get the courage to walk inside."

Oh, he could understand that. In all honesty, he hoped she didn't want him to sit in the chair next to her.

"Okay," he said, clapping his hands and facing the front door to the tattoo parlor. "You want me to shove you in?"

"No." She giggled. "Just… give me a minute."

He tilted an eyebrow. Was she really considering getting a tattoo? It seemed so far down the list of things she wanted to defeat that he didn't think she'd go for it. He had to admit, he was impressed she was even outside the door.

Her fingers twitched, and she slipped a hand into her

pocket and pulled out a folded piece of paper. "I... Well, this has been in my room for a while." She handed it over, their skin brushing. "I thought it was time to... I mean... I think I'm ready for it to be on my body. And not in momentary ink."

"May I?" he asked, holding up the paper. She nodded, and he unfolded it, being careful with the aged page. Pencil dust covered most of the edges and immediately stained the pads of his thumbs. A small smile teased the corner of his mouth, and he flicked his gaze to hers.

"Where were you thinking of putting it?" he asked.

"Um..." She looked up and down the street, then stepped into him, using him as a shield from the traffic behind them. Her fingers curled into the hem of her pink sweater, pulling it up so slowly Steven could hardly remember to breathe. "I was thinking here," she whispered, running her thumb over the bare skin of her hip. Steven swallowed, his brain short-circuiting.

"That... Uh... Well, I..." What was he saying? He blinked, the muscles in his hands cramping from the energy it took to keep them to himself. He let his gaze drift across her skin, up the bunched material around her bra line, over her exposed collarbone, and then finally meeting her nervous honey eyes.

"Steven?" she asked, and he shook himself out of it. Her sweater fell back into place, and she tucked her hands into her sleeves. "You don't think it's a good idea, do you?"

He jerked back. "Why do you think that?"

She lifted a shoulder. "I don't know. You're rarely

speechless. Unless you're trying to spare feelings."

Wow… she said that with absolute confidence. She was right; his tongue had never been as tied as it was around her.

"It'll probably hurt a lot," she mused, a nervous shadow crossing her eyes as she looked up at the tattoo sign. "Maybe I should pick a different spot. Like my arm or thigh… or breast… or something."

She was killing him, and he focused on a dead leaf on the sidewalk so his mind didn't run with all the visuals that had flipped through his head.

"I think your hip is perfect," he said. "It's going to hurt no matter what, so why not get it where you really want it?"

"Good point," she said with a breathy laugh. "And you don't think the tattoo is… Well… stupid? Or cliché?"

"I don't think it should matter what I think."

Her eyes fell to her hands, and she tugged on her hat strings again. "I… I do."

His chest tightened, and he nearly grabbed her face and kissed the tip of her nose, the apples of her cheeks, those plush lips… She cared what he thought? That wasn't something that someone said if they were only pretending, was it?

"Well, in that case," he said, his mouth pulling into a grin. "I think it's a beautiful tattoo, and it sure as hell makes me curious about you. And about what you want in life."

"Maybe I'll tell you," she said, a cute wrinkle appearing above her nose. "But first… you know… I have to get through the doors."

He held his hand out, palm up, and waited for her to

take it. She let out a musical laugh and slipped her fingers through his. Her body squeezed tight against his arm, and he was suddenly Superman, Batman, the entire Justice League. He was the luckiest man alive.

She followed his lead into the small shop, the door a bit heavier than he anticipated as he swung it open. She let out nervous laughter when he struggled with it and ducked under his arm to get inside before it slammed shut.

"...seriously, you can't be inking someone up if you've got a fractured wrist. How many times do I gotta tell you?" A girl with a round face and short red hair appeared from the back, scolding someone over her shoulder.

"It's my left one, Rae," a male voice answered. "My mad skills aren't going to be affected in the least bit."

The girl rolled her eyes, letting them land on Ginny and Steven. "Don't worry," she told them. "I'll keep his broken bones far away from your skin." She raised her voice and called over her shoulder, "No one wants your second rate work!"

"Ye of little faith." The owner of the second voice finally appeared, a bright blue cast covering his left wrist. He greeted them both—but especially Ginny—with a friendly grin and a head nod. "What can we do for you guys?"

"Well," Ginny started. "We were—"

"Oh! Are we doing a couple's tattoo today?" Rae's face lit up, her blue eyes skating between the two of them. "We've got a crapton of couple choices, unless you have something in mind."

She pushed a tablet across the counter, the screen open

to different art shots of his and hers tattoos. Steven could practically feel the heat radiating off Ginny's cheeks.

"Um… actually—"

"Dude, what if they aren't even together?" The guy waved his hand out at the two of them.

"You did not just call me dude." Rae put a hand up on her waist, her fingers pulling at the black fabric of her t-shirt. "And hello… they're holding hands."

Steven and Ginny both looked down as if they'd just become aware of the connection. Ginny had a way of making him nervous and comfortable all at once. Reaching for her hand was nerve-wracking, but once her palm was against his, it felt like the most natural thing in the world.

Ginny's lips turned up into a smile, and she met his eyes briefly before turning back to the bickering shop employees. "We're actually just here for me."

The guy pushed Rae back, sliding smoothly across the counter. "Tommy at your service," he said, and Steven squeezed Ginny's hand a little tighter. It wasn't like he owned her or had any claim on her, but he wanted her to know he really didn't want to go anywhere, no matter how many guys paid her attention.

"Hi," she said softly.

"Any idea what you what? Where you want it?" he said. Rae huffed behind him and leaned against the orange wall. He couldn't blame her. Was he really planning on tattooing someone with a broken hand?

"I do," she said, shooting a timid glance at Steven. As much as he'd like to help her out, he had to keep quiet and let her steer this ship. He was more than willing to offer silent comfort, and he stepped in closer to her, letting her hand go and wrapping an arm around her waist.

"Great," Tommy said, swiveling the tablet in front of him. He hit a few buttons then pulled a stylus out. "Let me hear 'em."

Ginny fiddled with the paper in her hand, and Steven eyed her movements as they crept toward her pocket.

"She's drawn something up," he said, running a comforting hand across her upper back. "You mind taking a look at it?"

Rae pushed off the wall and stuck her hand out. Ginny tentatively slid the drawing across the counter.

"Hey," Rae said, her lips curling up. "This isn't bad." She pointed a nail across the page. "What do you think of adding some flying pages on this book?"

Ginny perked up. "I... I think I'd like that."

"And maybe more of a 3D effect for the words, like they are coming from your skin and not sitting on top of it?"

Ginny nodded, that bright light that was so uniquely hers sparkling from her eyes.

"Where are you thinking of putting it?" Rae asked, sliding the page over to Tommy for him to take a look. Steven held his breath, bracing for another peek at Ginny's hip, but she kept her sweater down, only pushing a palm against the spot. Was she so comfortable with him that she felt okay showing him her bare skin?

He didn't want to overthink it, and he continued rubbing circles on her back. It wasn't just for her; he sure as hell needed the contact.

"I think we can do that," Rae said, leaning an arm on the counter and giving Tommy a look. "You got this, one-armed Joe?"

"Um... actually." Ginny's voice diminished when they turned their eyes on her. "I was... Well... Do you mind doing it?" she asked Rae.

Steven suppressed a laugh as Rae gave Tommy a smug grin and took the drawing. "Gladly," she told her. "Have a seat in the back, and I'll be there in a quick second."

They headed past the counter and through an open doorway, Ginny's shoulders moving up and down in silent laughter as Tommy and Rae bantered like childhood friends. It might've reminded Steven once of Cassidy and himself, but those days seemed so long ago he wasn't even sure if they were real or all in his head.

Ginny hopped in the chair, blowing out calming breaths and twisting her fingers together. She slid her hat off, static cracking around them, and her hair flew every which way. Steven grinned and pulled a chair up next to her.

"Doing okay?" he asked.

"Yes. No. Maybe."

"Anything I can do?"

She stuck her hand out. "Don't let go?"

twenty

The buzz of the tattoo gun rang through the room, and Ginny wiped a stray tear from her cheek. On the edge of her peripheral, she could see Steven move in close.

"You okay, Gin?" he asked. She pushed her tissue against her eye. She was getting a tattoo—never in her life had she thought she'd have the guts to do it, and there she was, in the chair, needle pressing in and out of her skin, with Steven's hand in hers.

"Distract me?" she asked, turning on the headrest. Her eyes locked with those ocean blues and shock ricocheted in her chest. There was such fear in his gaze, such concern. She squeezed his hand, trying to reassure him that even though there were tears, she wasn't exactly in pain. More like getting through it to come out the person she wanted to be.

Steven rested his chin on the chair near her shoulder. A puppy was gazing at her, and she wanted to reach out and touch him. There was no doubt he worked with animals.

"Feel like telling me what it means?" he asked, gesturing to her hip. Rae paused for a moment, wiping her forehead and stretching. It'd been a good hour or two, and Ginny's feet were definitely way past asleep, so she took the quick break to wiggle her legs awake before tilting back to a good spot for Rae to keep working.

Steven hadn't let go of her hand once.

"Did I tell you… about you know… wanting to be a therapist?" she asked.

"A little." His dimple popped up. "Not much, though."

"It's the whole reason I want to be… better."

"Better is debatable," he said, catching her off guard. "But continue."

She looked down at the gun as Rae pressed it against her skin. A wince pulled at her brows, and she focused on Steven. "My goal is to one day help people. I know it's going to be a hard career, especially for someone like me where I have to be sure of myself and in the advice I give, but… I'm a good listener, I think. And I have some experience with… you know… feelings of failure." She sucked in a breath through her teeth, a slice of pain shooting from her hip into her brain. Her hand tightened around his, and he scooted even closer. Any more and he'd be lying on the chair with her.

"You plan on going back to school then?" he asked, smartly pulling her back into the conversation.

She nodded. "If I can afford it. It's why I need that promotion. Why I need to get over my fears. Not just for the money, but to use my own experiences to help others." She gulped, eyes drifting toward the tattoo just as Rae finished the E. "To inspire."

She'd never said her ambitions out loud before, embarrassment and fear halting her from ever voicing it. She imagined someone laughing at her, or telling her that such a shy person couldn't possibly become a therapist. She'd thought those things so many times that she was sure that whenever she admitted it, whoever she told would validate her fears immediately.

Steven's dimples appeared, and he brought their joined hands up to his lips. He kissed each one of her knuckles, and the buzz surrounding her was no longer from a tattoo gun.

"You're going to be a pro at inspiring others, Gin. You inspire me on a daily basis."

If she didn't have a needle to her hip, her arms would've flown around his shoulders. A high-pitched squeal filled the room, and her brows scrunched as she looked for the source.

Rae's lips were pursed so hard Ginny would've guessed she was drawing blood. Her eyes lifted to meet Ginny's, and a small blush crept over her skin.

"Sorry," she said. "You guys are just really cute."

Ginny looked to Steven, and they let out a synchronized laugh. At least they could pull off the couple thing, but the only scary part was she was hardly pretending anymore.

Thanksgiving was just three nights, two days away. Ginny probably wouldn't see Steven for longer than a few minutes at a time before then, what with long hours of work ahead of them both. There was still so much to go over; her list of questions for him was sadly forgotten, and panic rose in her and pushed at the tattoo needle. If she was ever going to pass as Steven's girlfriend, she needed more than holding his hand and knowing his favorite color.

"All right," Rae said, straightening up with a smile. She

clicked the tattoo gun back into its holster. "What do you think?"

A sharp ache ran up Ginny's spine as she sat up, and a hiss went through her teeth. A back massage sounded good for about two seconds, and then she remembered how much touching that required and thought otherwise.

She pulled her sweater to the side, getting a better look at the fresh ink on her cherry skin. In the calligraphy letters, the word *Inspire* gleamed up at her, a book with flying pages wrapping around the *I* while the rest of the letters sat on a plush couch. The shading Rae had added made the whole thing look as if the words were actually coming from inside of her.

Ginny swiped at her cheeks with her crumpled up tissue. "I love it," she said. "Thank you."

"It's pretty darn beautiful," Rae said, grabbing a tube of some kind of ointment or lotion. "You had a great sketch to go off of. Inspiring, one would say." She winked, then blobbed the lotion on, and Ginny flinched as the ice cold cream hit her raw skin.

"Okay," Rae said, "you're going to want to put this on every morning and night. Make sure you clean the tattoo several times a day with soap and water and pat it dry. You can take the bandage off in about two or three hours, but not before then, got it?"

Ginny frowned; they had to cover it up so quickly. She'd like to stare at it all night. "How long will it take to heal?"

"If you take care of it, two to four weeks."

Steven shifted, his hand leaving hers for only a second to grab his phone out of his pocket. But he snatched it back once he'd opened his camera app. "Can I get a picture before you cover that up?"

Rae rolled out of the shot, and Steven zoomed in. Ginny hoped he wasn't getting her face in there, or that it didn't look like some more private body part. His smile widened when he checked the picture, then he turned the screen around so she could see.

"It's so pretty." A tiny squeal sat on the back of her tongue. "Will you send it to me?"

"Already done," he said, and her pocket vibrated. Rae bandaged her up, she paid for a job well done, then they headed out into the cool night air.

"I did it," she said softly, not really speaking to anyone but herself, but Steven turned his ocean gaze on her, and something close to pride resonated in those dimples. It was a direct shot of courage to her heart, and her feet bounced, her fingers squeezing his. "I did it!"

"Damn right, you did," he said, their shared joy wrapping around her like a bubble. She sucked in a breath, taking in the sweetness of this moment. Her hip was sore, for sure, but her pride was overwhelming every part of her.

"Thank you," she said, and she took the plunge and gave him an airtight hug. His hands slid around her, like they always did, like they had always meant to hold her. "I was having kind of a... crappy day." She wasn't even that embarrassed about what had happened with Alex earlier. Well... not as much anyway.

"Me too," he said, his voice low and warm in her neck. She pulled away, the heels of her boots going back on the pavement.

"Are you okay now?"

"Much better now, yeah." He pushed her hair from her face, tucking it into her hat. "You?"

"Definitely."

"You hungry?"

She nodded, even though she wasn't that hungry, but she wasn't in the mood to let go of him just yet.

"Oh!" she said, stopping him from taking her down the sidewalk. "Cocoa's probably worried. I haven't been home for a while and—"

"We can pick up something on the way home. Eat it on the porch or in the backyard?"

"O-okay." It was chilly, but hopefully he'd keep her warm.

He gave her a half grin. "I promise I won't make you cook for me again."

"Probably for the best."

They started down the walk, Ginny following his lead since she had no idea if he drove or they were waiting for an Uber or what. They approached Grandpa Atkinson's Cadillac, and Steven opened the creaky door for her.

"Man," he said with a shake of his head as she plopped into the passenger seat. He gazed at her, awe in his eyes.

"What?" she asked.

He let out a sigh. "I'm just really impressed by you, Gin. You talk about not being brave, but you just did something I don't have the guts to do." He ran a hand through his black hair, and the strands fell back into a perfect mess. "You should give yourself more credit."

Heat fired in her face, and he shut the door and came around. She pushed her cold fingers against her cheeks, hoping to calm down the inferno. He would probably never know just how much his words meant to her.

***

Ginny twisted a lo mein noodle around her finger and dangled it over Cocoa's eager nose.

"You want some?" She used the voice reserved for the cutest of dogs. "You have to say please."

A whine came from the back of Cocoa's throat, and she eased up on her hind legs. Ginny dropped the noodle into the pup's mouth, praising her with lots of "Good girls."

"You've had her for what? Four days and she's already doing that?" Steven waved his hand out at the injustice. "My darn dogs still think my shoes are kibble."

She covered a laugh, swallowing her mouthful of Chinese noodles. "But they're cute. And you're a pushover."

He playfully gasped. "Am not."

"Are to."

"Okay, you're right."

They laughed, and Ginny settled her half-gone bowl on the couch cushion and shimmied up to Steven's side. It was only for warmth, even though he'd set a nice space heater on the porch for them. She couldn't keep from touching him in some capacity nowadays. Next week was going to be rough.

"So…" she said, lifting a leg onto the couch and playing

with the fuzzy slippers Grandpa Atkinson loaned her cold toes. "How did we meet?"

"Huh?" he asked, noodle hanging from the side of his mouth. It was completely unfair that he still looked good as he slurped it up.

"At dinner Thursday." She pushed her finger at the fuzz on her slipper. "That's usually the first thing people ask couples, right? How they met?"

"Okay... Your point?"

She let out a huff. "Well, how did we meet? Was it some super hero story where you rescue me from oncoming traffic? Or do we say we met online so that there aren't any backup questions? Or what about I came in to adopt Cocoa... Oh, that wouldn't work. Cassidy was there—"

"Gin..." He set a hand on her knee. He put his food to the side and turned to face her, his leg up flush against hers. "We don't have to lie about any of that. I... I actually like our story."

She jerked back, her brows pinching. "And... well, I mean... what *is* our story?"

He let out a soft chuckle that sent goosebumps rampant across her skin. His eyes fell to his hand on her knee, and he ran his thumb over her leggings.

"There I was," he said, lifting his gaze, "standing over a pot of mac and cheese. And I thought, damn... I'm out of milk."

A smile teased the corners of her mouth, and she bit it away, embarrassed by his sweetness.

"I had nowhere to turn," he continued with dramatic

flair. "Nowhere to go. What was I to do? Then I remembered… Jemma was at book club. I could go over and ask in the most gentlemanly manner I possessed for someone to please rescue my dinner."

Ginny shook her head, almost ready to refute him. That day wasn't the first time they'd met, but she liked this story, too. It suited them.

"So I cross the street, bringing my lucky puppies for some sympathy, and what do you know… I was gobsmacked by the most gorgeous woman I'd ever laid eyes on."

"Stop it," she said, unable to stop her cheeks from flaming.

"It's true." He put a hand over his heart. "She was gorgeous. And when I asked her for a third cup of milk, she came back with half a gallon and told me to take it. Her heart was even more beautiful than her face, which believe me, I didn't think possible."

His hand ran circles over her knee, and he stopped, pinching the fabric between his thumb and forefinger. Ginny didn't understand why her mouth was watering so hard, why her heart was a foreign beat in her ears, why that simple touch was melting her to the core. But it was, and she didn't want to run from all those scary feelings. She was ready to plunge headfirst into them if it meant Steven would touch and talk to her like this again.

"I think we know enough about each other, Gin. And I don't want to lie."

But the whole thing was a lie, wasn't it? Her forehead wrinkled, and she tried to process exactly what he wanted from her, but she couldn't wrap her head around it. Pretending to be his girlfriend wouldn't be so hard at least on her side of things.

A buzz cut through the tension, and Ginny jerked out of her thoughts and reached for her phone.

"It's... Well, it's my work," she said.

"You can take it." Steven pushed from the couch and gathered their garbage. He headed inside to his barking pups while Cocoa snagged his spot.

"Hello?" she answered, hoping her voice didn't sound as broken and confused as she felt.

"Hi, I'm looking for a Ginny Thompkins."

"This is she."

"This is Katrina Watkins from Mill's Industries human resources. I have your resume for a position at his advertising company?"

She took a deep breath. "Yes. I was interested in moving departments."

"You work in Mail and Delivery?"

"Yes."

"We'd like to set up an interview with you. Is there a day or time next week that works?"

An interview? This was it; she was getting to that next step, and she wasn't sure how she was going to handle it from here. She grabbed her stomach, wincing at the sting from her tattoo she'd already forgotten about.

"Um... I... Well, I can usually do Monday afternoons."

"Perfect. Let's set you up for a three o'clock on this coming Monday after the holiday. Does that sound okay?"

"Mmmhmm." Words were going to fail her if she used them.

"I have you penciled in. I can't wait to meet with you."

"Thank you."

She hung up, her hand shaking from adrenaline. What a rush the night had been, and she wasn't even tired.

Cocoa crawled into her lap and snuggled, calming her nerves a bit. Now she had a focal point besides Steven and Thanksgiving, and thank heavens she did. She wasn't sure how much longer she would be able to keep her feelings hidden from him.

twenty-one

Steven tossed and turned on his mattress, his feet pushing against the weight of one of his puppies. He huffed into his pillow and squinted at his fitness watch.

Four AM. He'd slept all of three hours, and not all at once. It was completely out of the ordinary for him. His body was on a strict internal clock, in bed at ten and up at six, but every time he dozed off, he startled awake a few minutes later; he was so on edge.

He shoved his blankets off, stood, and stretched. Batman stirred in his sleep; but both puppies slept like Steven hadn't just launched out of bed. Good, he didn't want the self-imposed guilt trip of going for a run without them.

He grabbed his new running shoes, some sweats, and a light jacket, then crept out the front door. The morning was a crisp one, fog spread over the street, a subtle mist in the air. Steven sucked in the scent of Thanksgiving, of pumpkins and leaves and family. His breath clouded over him, and he finished his stretches.

The week had gone by so fast he could hardly believe it was already Thursday. The shelter had been buzzing, what with Cat Craze happening. Every November, they had an adoption sale on older cats. And by sale, they were giving waiving all adoption fees. It was unfortunate that most adoptions were for puppies and kittens, but understandable. The entire litter of tuxedo kittens had already gone to good homes, but many of the older cats who'd been there for so long were passed right on by.

It was the hardest part of his job—resisting the urge to take them all. Every animal sitting in a kennel broke his heart, but he was grateful Cat Craze was going well so far. The older cat numbers had definitely slimmed, but it was a crap deal that for every cat that got adopted, more came in the door.

He took a deep breath and broke into a jog, eyeing Ginny's window as he passed. He wondered if she knew how rare it was for the timid dogs to get adopted. How she probably saved Cocoa's life from a kennel. It was just another thing that had drawn him in.

That was the main thing keeping him awake—Ginny, him, what they were or what they weren't. When he'd asked her to pretend, the thought of falling for her never crossed his mind. He was so wrapped around the one that got away that he hadn't been open to any other possibility. Then Ginny stepped into his life and turned it upside down. So slowly, that he didn't even notice just how much he liked her until he was deep in.

He pushed out his breath and sucked it in, the rhythm in tune with each step against the rained down pavement. He was never good at expressing how he truly felt, Cassidy just one prime example. What if Ginny laughed at him? No... she wouldn't laugh. She might get embarrassed, that adorable blush covering her cheeks as she squeaked out a timid rejection. She'd remind him that he was in love with someone else not two weeks ago, that she deserved more than a rebound.

She did deserve more than that. But was she a rebound? Or was she exactly what he'd been looking for?

***

"I don't see why I can't drive my own damn car," Grandpa huffed from the passenger seat. Steven gave him the side-eye, then looked in the rearview to catch Ginny's reaction. Her lips pursed, biting back a laugh as she looked out her window and stroked Cocoa in her lap. Her hair was curled, the turquoise ends especially vibrant against a gray and black sweater that hugged her curves, but hung loose around her waist. Her tattoo was most likely uncovered now and healing. Steven could still envision it with perfect clarity.

"Because we want to make it to the Joanes' house in one piece, Grandpa," Jemma teased, leaning up from the back and resting her chin on Grandpa's seat. He groaned, crossing his arms and glaring out the window.

"Been drivin' for sixty years with no accidents. Not a darn ticket. You young people and your crazy notions that old people can't drive. When I was your age I damn well respected my elders."

"Didn't you set your grandpa's cabin on fire?" Steven asked. Jemma's eyes widened, and she nodded an enthusiastic agreement.

"Yeah, well... that was different."

The most beautiful laugh floated through the air, and it captured all of their attentions, but especially Steven's.

Ginny's face reddened when all eyes turned on her, and she quickly sputtered, "You're just... You guys are just... Fun."

Jemma snorted. "Even the grumpy old man, here?"

"Yes," Ginny said, her face still the color of a ripe tomato. "He did reintroduce me to leaf jumping."

The smallest of smiles wrapped up Grandpa's face. "Come 'round my place when snow sticks for more than a day. We'll do some sledding."

"In your front yard?"

"Oh, it can be done," he said, his grumpiness almost completely faded. Steven grinned and got on the freeway, enjoying the laughter and banter Ginny was now a part of. She fit so well with them.

He pulled up to the Joanes' place about ten minutes later, the tire bumping against the curb. He got a "Ha!" from Grandpa, and they all climbed out with a pie. Ginny held one that looked extremely legitimate as homemade, and he was tempted to ask her if she didn't go store bought like the rest of them.

His steps fell heavy against the drive as they made their way to the front door. Ginny stood close, Cocoa in step right alongside her, wagging her tail. Steven set a hand on the small of her back. Touching her was so comfortable and nerve-wracking all at once it was hard to pin down how it truly felt other than... perfect.

"You ready for this?" he asked, leaning down to her ear. Shock danced in her honey eyes.

"Me?" she said. "W-what about... I mean, how are you doing?"

"I'm good." And he was. "But I should warn you, Cassidy's mom can be a bit—"

"Steven!" a loud cry came from the front porch, breaking them apart. Ms. Joanes bounded down the steps, pushing everyone out of the way to get her arms around him. "Praise Jesus, when Cassidy said you might not be comin', I got so mad. You don't do that to me, you got it?"

"Yes, ma'am."

"Ma'am." She stepped back with a laugh. "I give you hell and you're still a damn gentleman."

She patted his cheek and then turned to greet Grandpa and Jemma. Ginny's brows rose, and she looked to Steven for help.

"Oh, you haven't seen the worst of this woman," he whispered, and a playful fear rose in her eyes. He laughed and kissed her forehead, the action so natural to him he hadn't realized he'd even done it until Ms. Joanes tilted her head in his direction.

"Who's this?" she asked, pointing at Ginny. Her eyes fell to the now nervous dog resting between Ginny's legs. "And that?"

"Cassidy told you I was bringing someone, right?"

Ms. Joanes' jaw clenched. "She might've mentioned it. I thought she was joking about the dog, but…" She shook her head then stuck her hand out. "Naomi Joanes. You are…?"

"Um… Ginny."

"Are you not sure?"

"Hey," Grandpa piped in. "You be nice to Ginny. She's the sweetest thing since cotton candy."

Naomi waved him off. "I was only teasing. Nice to meet you, Ginny. Come on in. Don't kick my pumpkins; I spent hours painting those suckers."

Stepping into the Joanes' living room was like diving into a time machine. Everything looked the same as it always did around this time of year. Naomi liked to go all-out for every holiday, and she was not one to skip Thanksgiving for the sake of Christmas. The painted pumpkins were just the beginning. The scent of maple hung in the air; orange, brown, and yellow candles surrounded by fake leaves sat on nearly every side table and on the mantle. The dining table was decked out with turkey-themed flatware, and a large cornucopia sat on the kitchen island. Ginny's face lit up as she took it all in, and Steven's mouth twitched. He didn't know her favorite holiday yet. Was this it? He couldn't imagine her not having any plans on her favorite holiday.

"Where's the Joanes' crew?" Jemma asked, hanging her jacket up on the hook by the door.

"Adam and Ben should be here any second, and Cassidy is upstairs showing her boyfr—I mean, Jon, her old bedroom."

It wasn't lost on Steven the sudden distaste in Naomi's tone, but to his surprise, it actually made him sad. Cassidy had enough drama with her parents. Adding disapproval of her boyfriend would only stir the already messy pot.

Though, it wasn't out of the ordinary for Cass's mom. She wasn't too fond of her sons' choice in partners either. According to her, it would be better to be alone than with someone who would inevitably cheat on you. And with her background, Steven supposed he could hardly blame her for that line of thinking.

The front door creaked open, and the booming voice of Cassidy's oldest brother, Adam, greeted them.

"Happy Thanksgiving!"

Two little versions of Adam bolted into the room, climbing up on the couch and jumping in full winter gear. Ginny lifted her hand and covered her sweet laugh, and Steven pulled her close. "I'll take that to the kitchen," he said, snagging the pie. "You good for a minute?"

She nodded, and he took the desserts into the heavenly smelling kitchen. The turkey was roasting in the oven, a pan of potatoes rested on the counter, and he resisted the urge to pick from the bowl of stuffing.

He pushed the pies into the fridge, shuffling things around so they'd fit.

"Hey! You're here." The distinct voice of his childhood sweetheart echoed around him, and he peered around the fridge door with a hopefully friendly grin.

Cassidy looked as cute as ever, her glasses resting on her fresh face, her brown hair tied up into a high ponytail. She wore a blue tank top under a half jacket with the Iron Man emblem stitched on the pocket.

Steven's gaze moved from her to the tall, couldn't miss him, man standing next to her. He was definitely older, but probably not by too much. His blond hair was showing signs of gray on the side, and his eyes said he'd been up late the night before. His face was friendly, though, and his hand was tucked into Cassidy's comfortably.

She smiled and gave Steven a side hug. "You finally get to meet." She stepped back and squeezed her man's arm. "Jon, this is Steven. Steven, Jon."

They shook hands, and a possessive string yanked on Steven's stomach. How was she so happy with him? Did he know a thing about Marvel movies? Or did he hang out and watch her deduce brain teasers for fun? Did he buy her cardboard stand-ups or did he make her get rid of them?

Steven crossed his arms and nudged the fridge door shut with his elbow. "So, how'd you guys meet?" he said, his voice clipped.

Cassidy let out a laugh and pinched Jon's side. "Told you he was going to be worse than my brothers." She gave Steven a look. "We work together. Jon's a doctor at the OB clinic."

"An OB?"

"Yes. He brings life into the world, so you can't find a negative thing about that, all right." She let out a sigh, and Steven forgot how easy it was for her to say exactly how she felt. Ginny was rarely like that, so when he did hear it, it felt like a prize somehow.

"Sorry," he said, shaking his head and then offering up a friendly grin to Jon. "Just a habit. Make sure my best friend got a good one, you know?"

Jon held up a hand. "I get it, no worries." He checked over his shoulder. "And no offense, but I'm more terrified of her mom."

Steven laughed. "As you should be."

Adam came around the corner with Ben in tow. He

tossed a football across the room, and Steven easily caught it.

"Turkey bowl time," Adam said, pointing at Steven. "You're going down this year."

Steven half-smiled, then tossed the ball to Jon who let go of Cassidy's hand to catch it. "I got dibs on the doc," he said, and the joy on Cassidy's face was worth it. Only problem now was he wasn't sure if he was being the nice guy because that's who he was, or if he was being nice because he was ready to move on. Either way seemed okay.

twenty-two

Ginny huddled into the soft fabric of Steven's jacket and breathed in the clean scent that was distinctly his. Cassidy sat next to her in the loveseat styled camp chair, wrapping herself up in a blanket she took from Jon's car.

"Look at you two," Jemma said from her bright red camp chair set up on Cassidy's other side. Cocoa perched in Jemma's lap, enjoying the new company. "Sniffing your guy's clothes like you wanna get high on it."

"Maybe I do," Cassidy quipped, then she took another exaggerated whiff of the blanket. Ginny smiled at their antics, secretly wishing she was as bold as they were. From what she'd learned of Cassidy in the short little while they'd been watching the guys play football, she was smart and beautiful, and she had a cute charm that played in her favor when it came to the opposite sex. She was also extremely passionate about her Marvel movies, and was very disappointed that Ginny hadn't seen a single one.

"Hey, Ginny," Cassidy said, shifting in her seat to face her. "Where did you get your hair done?"

"Um... I..." She gulped and ran her fingers over her curls. It had taken her a good hour to get her whole head done up, but she wanted to look nice for Steven. She hardly ever got the chance to dress up for something. "I did it myself."

"For real?" Cassidy reached for a handful and examined the bright blue Ginny had touched up for the occasion. "It looks amazing."

"Ginny is crazy amazing at all sorts of crap," Jemma said, taking a sip from her Coke. Surprise tied Ginny's tongue, and she shook her head in silence.

"Oh, come on," Jemma said. "No need to be humble about it." Her gaze skipped over Ginny and fell to Cassidy. "She does these awesome temporary tattoos, and she even designed the real one she just got on her hip, and her makeup is practically flawless every day, and she trained this dog within like, a day."

Ginny's face blazed, and she glared across the field to big-mouthed Steven. His shirt was off—he was on the "skins" team—and sweat beaded his forehead and ran down the line of his back. How much had he told his sister about her? Did Jemma know that he was Ginny's first kiss? Did she know the whole thing was a ruse?

Ginny held her arms out to take Cocoa back to help her calm down. Her pup bounced on over and gave her cheek a good lick.

"You just got a tattoo?" Cassidy pointed to the field. "Jon's cousin owns a tattoo shop downtown. Tommy's Tats."

"That's... that's where I went."

A bright smile lit up Cassidy's face. "Did Rae do it for you? Thomas' arm is busted up right now, which is why I ask."

Ginny bit her lip. "I... Well, I mean... We designed it together. She had some really great... um, you know... ideas."

"I was thinking about getting one I wouldn't regret," Cassidy said, holding up her forefinger. A black mustache was printed in her skin, and she pushed it under her nose for effect.

"I don't know." Ginny grinned. "I kinda like it."

"You are the only one." She waved at Jon on the field, who was also shirtless. Colorful, Disney tattoos covered his back. "Well, except him. But he could be lying his cute butt off because we're in the 'first stage' of dating."

"He's definitely lying," Jemma said, and they laughed together while Cassidy chucked her empty Coke bottle at Jemma's face. Ginny stroked Cocoa's fur and relaxed into the seat. It was nice, just being there, chatting with near strangers. A few weeks ago, the thought alone would've put her into panic mode.

"Hey, you girls wanna play?" Ben asked from the sideline. Grass stains and dirt covered his shirt, and sweat dripped trails into the dirt on his face. His smile was bright white, though.

"But we're having so much fun ogling Jon shirtless," Jemma called back, much to the doctor's—and Ginny's—embarrassment. Cassidy wolf-whistled, and Jon swiped his shirt off the grass and pulled it over his head.

Ginny eyed Steven and secretly hoped his shirt stayed put on the ground.

"I... I'll play," Ginny squeaked, settling Cocoa into the

chair as she got up. All the guys cheered as she made her way over and pulled her hair up into a ponytail. Her heart pounded with every step. She'd played with strangers before, and if she played opposite Steven, there was a chance of his arms wrapping around her again.

Steven stood straight, something a lot like pride emanating from his smile. He high-fived her as she stepped onto the field, and then playfully tapped her butt. A jolt like lightning lit her up and buzzed under her skin.

"G-guess I'm on the other team," she said, the exciting touch throwing her off balance a bit.

"Why's that?" he asked.

"Because I'm not playing skins."

The guys threw their heads back with laughter, and Ben waved her over to his and Adam's side. Jon reluctantly took his shirt off, and both Jemma and Cassidy cat-called him. Ginny could relate to the bright red blush going through his ears, and she wondered just how shy he was, too.

"Oh, all right." Cassidy got up from her spot. "Guess I'm in, too."

Jon grinned, straightening up. "Well, we need even numbers, so it's not shirts and skins anymore."

"Unless you want my shirt off," Cassidy teased, and both Adam and Ben shouted a resolute NO!

Jon put his shirt back on, and Steven lifted a brow and reached for his.

"Wait!" Ginny said, surprising herself with the outburst. Cocoa rustled on the chair, ears perking up like she was ready to run out to see what was wrong. A sheepish smile played at her lips, and she tilted her head. "I... um... don't want you to put that on just yet."

"Ooooooh," the two brothers said in unison. She covered her blush, but Steven dropped his shirt on the sideline and jogged back into position. He pushed a soft kiss to her cheek and winked.

Whoops... Did he think she only said that to play up her attraction to him? He should know by now she wasn't that great of an actress.

Her team had the ball, and Adam pulled them over to a huddle. The guys smelled like sweat and grass and football, and it reminded her of the frat boy game, bringing excitement back into her legs. She practically bounced while Adam called the shots, asking Ginny how good of a runner she was.

"I'm pretty fast," she admitted. "I outran Steven last time we played."

"Awesome. Ball goes to Gin."

They broke and met the other three on the line. Steven playfully eyed Ginny, mouthing, "I got you." She really hoped so.

"Down!" Adam yelled. "Set!"

"Time for food!" Ms. Joanes called from the back porch. The groans that echoed around the field surprisingly also came from Ginny. "Guys, wash up so you don't stink up my house."

The call of dinner had Adam and Ben bolting toward the house. Steven laughed, shaking his head.

"Guess you'll get me next time?" Ginny teased him. A

mischievous glint twinkled in his blue eyes, and she took off, knowing he was ready to chase her.

Giggles ran up and down her throat, and she ducked and dodged Steven's hands. Cocoa jumped onto the field, bouncing between them, and Steven finally got a hold of her wrist and pulled her in. His fingers relentlessly tickled her ribs, and she squealed, begging him to stop while simultaneously wishing he never would.

They paused, catching their breath, Ginny's smile so big that she was unsure it belonged to her. Steven's dimples were breathtaking, and his skin was slick beneath her hands. For the millionth time since she'd met him, she thought of how unfair it was for someone to look this beautiful and have such a kind soul. Her nails trickled up his chest and lightly scratched the underside of his chin. He was smooth today, like butter. Like when he'd kissed her.

"Ew, Ginny!" Jemma called out across the field. "Make him shower before you let him touch you."

The spell broken, Steven looked at her and let out a breathy laugh. His arms dropped, leaving her cold, but not empty.

"She does have a point." He bent down, picked Cocoa up with one hand, and handed the pup over. Then they made their way inside where the line for the showers was already three men deep.

***

"He's such a nice boy, isn't he?" Ms. Joanes said to Ginny while Steven sat at the bottom of the stairs, still waiting for a shower. Ginny couldn't imagine the water would be the least bit warm.

"Oh, Steve's the nice guy, all right," Adam said, his hair wet from the shower. He popped a grape into his mouth from the fruit bowl on the table. "It's why we creamed him out on the field."

Ben joined in the ribbing. "Yeah, you know what this nice guy did when his homecoming date cancelled on him sophomore year?"

Ginny shook her head and squeezed Cocoa to her chest.

"He drove her," Jemma piped in. "He drove her to the dance to meet up with another guy."

"She had him wrapped around that manipulative finger," Ben said with a laugh. "At least until he met that one." He jabbed a thumb at his sister in the adjoining living room.

"Like you guys don't have a woman calling the shots for you," Steven said from the stairwell. The guys all laughed and mocked him.

"You can make him do anything, can't you?" Adam nudged Ginny's arm. "He turns on the charm, but you hold the reins."

"Steven… Flirt?" Ben snorted around a cracker. "I bet he asked Ginny's parents politely before asking to court her."

"Yes, Mr. and Mrs. Ginny…" Adam put on an old English accent. "Might I trouble you for an evening of shakes and hand holding with your daughter?"

"We will promptly return at nine o'clock sharp," Ben

added. They bowed like a couple of idiots, and Ginny caught a glimpse of Ben's wife, Ada, mouthing an apology over his shoulder.

Steven sighed and ran a hand over his sweaty hair. A frown pulled at Ginny's lips. She wasn't familiar enough with the guys' dynamic to know if this truly bothered him or not, but she wasn't going to let them push him around because of his sweet soul. She liked it, found it… dare she say, sexy.

The water shut off upstairs, and Steven pushed to his feet. "If you guys are done, I'm gonna shower now."

"So polite, asking if we're done making fun of him before he leaves the room," Adam teased. In a split second decision, Ginny straightened her shoulders and passed Cocoa off to Jemma.

"I'll… I'll join you," she said, and before she could analyze the shock on Steven's face, she grabbed his hand and led him up the stairs. The girls all laughed at the guys, their voices growing distant as Ginny pulled Steven down the hall.

"You keep it clean in my house!" Ms. Joanes called up the stairs.

"Really, Mom?" Cassidy cackled. "Should we go over what happened at *my* house in *my* bed?"

They're voices faded, and Steven tugged Ginny to a stop.

"Hey," he whispered, turning to a room and nudging the door open. "In here for a second."

She followed him inside, her heart skipping as the door clicked shut behind her. A bed sat flush against the far wall, and posters of the Hulk and the red and gold metal guy hung above the headboard.

"So…" His voice tripped, which was very unlike him. "Are you actually… I mean, do you really want to shower with—"

"No!" she blurted, shaking her head. "I wasn't going to actually…" She let out an embarrassed laugh, rubbing her hands together. "They were just… you know… And you looked like you could use… I dunno."

"What?"

She took a deep breath and tried to piece together what she wanted to say. "It just seemed like maybe you wanted to… not be the nice guy for a minute."

"And showering with my girlfriend in someone else's home qualifies as… not nice?"

"A little naughty, yes." She pushed on her cheeks, hoping the cold of her fingers would fight against the warmth.

He stared at her for a moment, a foreign emotion passing over his handsome features. She held her breath, afraid she'd done the wrong thing, made the wrong move.

"I could… head back downstairs, if you want." Her gaze dropped to her twisting hands. "I was just going to wait for you to get out, maybe wet my hair so it looked like I was in there with you…"

"Gin," he said, his voice low. He shook his head and stepped into her space. "Why are you doing this for me?"

That was a good question, and the easy answer was that they had a deal. This was part of her job, wasn't it?

But it wasn't. She'd seen him uncomfortable, and she

wanted to stick it to those responsible. An inexplicable urge to protect him had come over her, and she was powerless to stop it.

Her lips parted, but no sound came out. How could she tell him how she felt when it was all pretend?

A click broke through the air, and panic seized her chest. The door behind her creaked open, and she leapt on Steven, grasping his face and pulling his mouth down on hers. If the ruse was to be believable, they had to be more than talking. But as his shock reverberated against her lips, scorching humiliation sank down on her.

"Oh, uh… Sorry…" Jon stuttered from the door, his hair wet, a towel wrapped around his torso. Ginny eased off of Steven, putting several feet of space between them.

Jon's ears were fire red, and he reached past Steven. "I just need to grab these…" he said, picking up a pile of clean clothes from the bed. "Don't let me interrupt."

He quickly exited, shutting the door behind him. Ginny refused to look Steven's way, a tie between amusement and embarrassment creeping through her stomach.

The room was too quiet. She could hear every beat of her heart, every conversation buzz from downstairs. Her face was flush, the air around her too hot to concentrate.

Just as she thought she'd combust from the silence, a strong but gentle hand snatched her wrist. Steven pulled her against him, his palm cupping her cheek as he pressed his urgent lips on hers.

twenty-three

Steven had never wanted someone as much as he wanted Ginny in that moment. After the initial shock, her body melted against his, and he hoisted her up, her legs wrapping effortlessly around his waist.

His tongue slid into her mouth, tangling with hers and lighting him up. He backed her into the door, a sexy moan of satisfaction rising from deep in her throat. He ate it up, kissing and touching this sweet girl from across the street. She matched him kiss for kiss, taste for taste, surprising him with her enthusiasm. Her nails scratched down his back, eliciting a beast-like groan from his chest.

He squeezed her thighs, adjusting her on his waist to better explore her with his hands. His fingers crept under her sexy sweater, her stomach jerking with the initial contact. She was soft, plush, gorgeous. He gripped her waist, careful to avoid the fresh tattoo. A pleased whimper fell from her kiss-swollen lips, and it sank into his heart and stole his breath away.

Her nails continued to cling and claw at his back, and he pushed at her sweater, urging it up her smooth, braless back, kissing her deep and fast like he'd wanted to all day. All week. Ever since he'd met her.

His mouth traveled down to her neck, pressing open-mouthed kisses to her pulse and the underside of her jaw. A thud echoed through the room as she tilted her head back, letting it hit the wooden door. He carefully took a step toward the bed, using only his strength to keep her up. He loved on her neck and slithered his hand around her waist, to the small of her back, then up her bare spine. Her skin was like honey, just like her—smooth and tempting to taste.

Her hands gripped his shoulders, and she squeezed, a satisfied breathy sigh leaving her gorgeous lips. He hardly cared that he was sweaty from the field, that he was most likely covered in dirt. The fact that she was responding to him this way instead of revulsion propelled him onward, and he kissed her again, tasting the corners of her mouth and reveling when her tongue returned the favor.

Was this really happening? He wanted to ask it, but her fingers tugged at the hair near the nape of his neck, and he lost all train of thought.

As scared as she seemed, she was as opposite as could be with her kisses. She gave them freely, with little to no hesitation. Their eyes met, and deep passion sang from her irises, and a smile hit his lips before he went in for more. She slithered her hands between their bodies and tucked her fingers into the hem of her sweater. Following her lead, he slipped it over her head and let it drop to the floor with a flump.

Her bare chest fell flush with his, and she wrapped her arms around his shoulders. He took a moment to let it all sink in, staring into her eyes as he tucked her hair behind her ear. This was far from fake; they both had to know that now.

She was the best thing that had happened to him in a very long time.

He kissed the tip of her nose, and she giggled, her face turning a beautiful shade of pink. She tussled his grimy hair, the bridge of her nose wrinkling.

"I've never been topless with a guy before," she said after a minute.

"Are you okay?" he asked. As comfortable as he was, he would help her back into that sweater the second she asked him to.

A small smile teased the corner of her mouth. She leaned down, pressing her lips to his briefly. "You make me feel okay."

"Me too," he said, then quickly clarified. "I mean about you."

She laughed, and he gave her a gentle, long kiss, sinking in her skin and her soul and her sweetness.

A tap came at the door, and he reluctantly drifted apart. "Yeah?"

"Sorry," Cassidy's voice muffled, annoyance resting on the edges of her tone. "But everyone's getting pretty anxious to eat."

He locked eyes with Ginny, and the most adorable pout pulled at her lips. He laughed and gently set her on her feet.

"Be down in a second," he told Cassidy. Guilt piled in his stomach as the room came back into focus. Cass had just caught her parents in her bed a month ago, and now her ex was making out in her childhood bedroom with another woman.

Ginny sucked in a breath then blew her hair from her face. She covered her chest and looked for her sweater. Steven swiped it up and helped her into it.

"I'm going to take a quick shower." He planted a peck on her lips. "You'd better not join me, because I want to keep it to five minutes."

She grinned, a playful glint in her eyes. "That's assuming I'd even want to shower with you."

He tapped her rear again as she opened the door, and she gleefully squealed, smiling down the hallway. She was fixing her shirt and hair until she disappeared from view. Steven took a breath, a little bit grateful that being last in line for the shower meant a cold one was in store for him anyway.

***

Steven bounded down the steps, clean, fresh, and ready to sit next to Ginny and hold her hand. When his feet hit the landing, a round of cheers sounded from the dining room.

"It's about time!" one of Adam's kids said from the kid table. "I'm *starving*."

"We all are, little buddy," Grandpa said, his grump look back on his face as he sat at the head of the table. Steven quickly took his spot next to Ginny, sliding in the chair and giving Naomi the go-ahead to start.

"Since we have some new faces this year," Naomi said, pointedly looking at Jon and Ginny, "I'll go over our Joanes-Atkinson tradition."

Grandpa harrumphed and spoke in a loud, speedy voice. "A long time ago we met and decided to have dinners together, and before eating we do the whole 'I'm grateful for' nonsense, and so I'll start. I'm grateful for Miss Ginny over there, because she's the only one who don't make fun of me for doing chores in my undergarments. Steven, you go."

Stifling a laugh, Steven set a hand on Ginny's leg under the table and squeezed her knee. "Same for me," he said. "But for different reasons."

Ginny nervously shifted in her seat, eyes darting to Naomi, who gestured her to go ahead.

"Um... I guess... I'm grateful for..." She bit her lip, and Steven traced finger hearts on her thigh, hoping they were more helpful than hindering.

"You can say Steven, you know," Jemma said from the other side of Grandpa. "We all know you guys are cheesy as hell."

A round of laughter went across the table, and Ginny gave him an apologetic look. "Um... I was actually going to say Cocoa."

Cocoa barked from the living room.

"Backseat to the dog." Adam laughed.

"Bitches before britches," Ben added.

"Ben!" Ada said, slapping his arm. "Kids are in the room."

The kids picked right up on the curse, and continued to say it until Grandpa threw a roll at them.

"Quiet! I'm hungry, and we have a million more gratitudes to go through."

The rest of the table hurried through what they were grateful for, none of them wanting to hear the wrath of

Grandpa. Jon said he was grateful for coding conferences and shared a secret look with Cassidy. Steven squeezed Ginny's leg again, surprised at how calm he was, how seeing those two together didn't affect him as much as he anticipated it would.

After Jemma, Grandpa dug into the turkey, not bothering to pass it around before taking a huge bite of the leg. Steven offered to dish out, and conversation buzzed around the table.

It had been a pretty drama-free Thanksgiving so far, knock on wood. Cassidy's dad wasn't there, which helped. He and Naomi were always back and forth with each other, arguing and sleeping together within the same few minutes, and then he would go off to find some other poor woman to torture. Naomi was a firm believer in love being some sort of sham, and with all of them—minus Jemma—getting paired off, he was bracing himself for a preachy anti-love sermon once the wine kicked in.

Steven could hardly keep his hand off Ginny's leg long enough to eat. His body was reeling from that kiss, and he couldn't wait to be alone with her again.

As soon as he was, he'd tell her how he felt. To think he'd spent the whole month dredging up the courage to confess to Cassidy when all of that changed in just a few short weeks. The feelings for Cass had fizzled down to what once was, and not what should be. Ginny was no rebound; she was the one he needed all along.

Her hand sneaked down from the table and tickled his wrist. They tangled their fingers together, and the food was forgotten and the conversation lost.

He leaned in close to her ear, whispering soft words against her skin. "Can I see you tonight?" he asked. Impatience had struck him, and he couldn't wait another second to solidify their after-dinner plans.

Ginny dropped her gaze and bit away a grin before whispering back, her breath sending a chill over his neck.

"It's tonight already, isn't it?" She peered over his shoulder to the darkening sky out the window.

"I meant after dinner, silly." He pinched her knee, and she jerked a bit. He'd have to remember that ticklish spot for future flirting. "Alone?"

Her eyes twinkled, and her lips parted to answer.

"Steven," Naomi said, her wine glass high in the air, the contents down to the last sip. She swayed a little as she pointed between him and Cassidy. "You think if you'd have opened your mouth a little sooner, it'd be you and my daughter whispering secrets to each other?"

Chatter came to a halt. Cassidy kicked under the table, and her mom gave her a dirty look.

"I'm just saying," Naomi continued. "He was all for asking you out at Halloween. Checking his phone all night, stopping by to see if you were around... Could've been a completely different dinner."

Cassidy shot a look down the table at Steven, who felt all the blood in his face drain. Ginny's hand slowly slipped from his, and he ran his palm across his jeans.

"Good thing I didn't." He tried to joke it off. "I would've had to play skins all by myself." He gestured to Jon who looked like he'd dry swallowed a large pill.

"You guys...?" Jon croaked, pointing a finger between Steven and Cassidy. Cassidy shook her head, knocking her glasses off center.

"They used to date, you know," Naomi said to her empty wine glass. "Pity they broke up, if you ask me. Think of how pretty their babies would've been."

"Mom," Cassidy warned. Steven reached for Ginny's hand, but it was nowhere to be found.

"What?" Naomi seemed genuinely confused about why Cassidy's eyes blazed anger. "Everyone knows Steven is only back home so he can win you over."

Cassidy's brows pinched together. "No... he's done with school. He's helping run the shelter. He's got a job and friends and a life. Not everything is about me, Mom."

Her eyes cast down the table to Steven, who didn't have time to compose himself. As soon as they locked gazes, the truth was impossible to hide. Cassidy's mouth popped open. "Right?" she asked him.

Steven took in every pair of eyes that turned his way, all except Ginny's. She stayed resolute, staring at her half-eaten dinner. His silence confirmed everything Naomi had drunkenly babbled, and before he could refute it, tell them it wasn't the case anymore, Ginny pushed from the table and gently set her napkin on top of her plate.

"I'm... Well, I'm pretty full," she said. "Would you like me to put this in the sink?"

"I'll go with you," Jon said, picking up his own plate. Cassidy eased from her chair, but he whispered something in her ear, and she sat back down. The two disappeared into the kitchen, and Cassidy hissed at her mom.

"Are you trying to ruin every relationship your children have? Or does it just come naturally."

Naomi waved her off. "He's fine. If he can't deal with you having ex-boyfriends, then he's not going to last very long."

"What about Ginny, huh?" Cassidy whisper-yelled. "Thanks for making that sweet girl uncomfortable."

"That 'sweet' girl was just in the shower with our Steven."

"He's not ours, Mom."

Steven grabbed the back of his head and pulled at his hair. Ginny was well aware of his feelings for Cassidy, but she wasn't aware of his feelings for her, and right now they trumped everything.

He shoved from his seat, tossing his napkin down and heading into the kitchen. Cocoa followed his lead, scampering off to find her owner.

"Hey," he said to Jon and Ginny, both at the sink. Jon washed their dishes, and Ginny dried. Steven faced Jon. "Could I have a second with my girl?"

It was painful how untrue that label was. He wanted it so much to be the truth, but he'd gone about this all wrong.

Jon dried his hands and left quietly.

"You okay?" he asked, even though he knew how stupid it was. Ginny placed the dry plates on the counter without turning around. She nodded, but her silence spoke volumes.

"Look, I know you knew about Cass and I, but things are... Well, they're different."

Cocoa rubbed up against Ginny's legs, and she made no movement to put the dog in her arms. She toyed with the dish towel, turning it over and over in her hands.

"It's okay, Steven," she said softly. "Like you said, I knew what this was."

"Gin..."

"We're fooling them all." She tossed the dish towel on the counter. "Had me fooled, too, for a minute there."

He crossed the room, grabbed her arm, and spun her around. Tears welled in her eyes, and his heart broke into a million pieces.

"If only you knew how wrong that is."

"None of it was real, Steven." She crossed her arms, shrugging from his hold. "We both got what we wanted, right? I have an interview on Monday, and Cassidy is completely convinced you're over her."

He jolted back. "You have an interview? Gin, that's great."

"Thanks." She finally leaned down and picked up her antsy pup. She held Cocoa close, her lips turned down into the fur. "So we don't need to keep the charade up," she said. "I can even find a ride home so you can stay and chat with Cassidy. Work things out between you."

"But—"

"You need to work it out, Steven."

She went to walk around him, and he grabbed her elbow, urging her to face him again. "Okay, okay," he said, panic squeezing his heart. "I promise I'll work things out with her. But I want to work things out with you, too."

Fear gripped her eyes, and she frowned, shaking her head. "There's nothing to work out. We're good."

But they weren't. She was going to walk out of his life believing that what they had was fake. He couldn't let her do that, but his hand slowly unraveled from her arm. She squeezed her dog and walked back into the business of Thanksgiving dinner.

twenty-four

Steven stood on his porch, waiting for any sign of Ginny to be home, but her house stood frustratingly dark, not even a porch light to give some indication that someone lived there.

He paced back and forth, checking his phone repeatedly for any missed messages or calls. He wanted to know her mind, her feelings on everything that happened today, including the kiss. There was no question that he'd fallen for her, but with how abruptly she left the car when they arrived back home, his paranoia was getting the better of him.

She'd gone inside for a moment, but he watched her put Cocoa in the basket of her bike and take off nearly an hour ago. He was ready to put up missing person signs.

An unfamiliar car pulled around the corner, and he perked up, his heart pumping as it stopped in front of the house.

Cassidy appeared from the backseat, and his heart sank, his feet back to their pacing. She scaled the porch steps and leaned against the railing, pushing her glasses into place.

"So," she said after a minute. "That was a fun day."

"Yeah." He allowed himself a little laugh, but it didn't make him feel any better. "I'll say."

"Is she mad?" she asked tentatively. Steven stopped

pacing, eyeing the house across the street.

"Honestly?" He slumped into the couch. "I have no idea."

Cassidy pushed off the railing and slouched next to him. "That's what conversations are for."

"I take it you and Jon already had yours?"

She nodded, kicking a leg up and resting her chin on her knee. Her chewed up nails picked at the frayed edges of her shoelaces. "He was a bit peeved I never told him that we'd dated. But it was ancient history." She turned her head, her knee now digging into her cheek. "At least... on my end."

He frowned and let out a sigh, his eyes still painfully on the dark house across the street.

"Was my mom spouting out horse crap?" Cassidy asked. "Or am I really the reason you came back to town?"

This was his chance to be honest with her—the moment he'd waited for but was never sure he'd be ready. Now that it was here, he couldn't care less. He wanted to run over to the clubhouse and see Ginny, if only she were there.

"At first," he admitted, meeting her eyes. "Cass, you meant a lot to me. I never wanted to break it off, but..."

"You did," she teased, and he shook his head with a laugh.

"I didn't want to do long distance, and for a while, I thought I'd made a huge mistake. Even up until Halloween I'd regretted that decision, but now?" He lifted a shoulder. "I love you, but not like I used to."

The corner of her mouth twitched. "Me too." Her brow

pinched, and she went back to picking her shoelaces. "So… if you were ready to be with me on Halloween, when exactly did you meet Ginny?"

Ah, now was where it got really tricky. He took a deep breath and gave her the side-eye. "You're gonna laugh at me."

She crossed her heart and zipped her lips. Even with that silent promise, he knew she'd make fun of him for making up a girlfriend.

He took her through last month, up to and including every kiss he'd shared with Ginny. He bragged about how she'd gotten a tattoo, how she'd braved the football field with a bunch of frat guys, how she burned a pie and still brought a homemade one to dinner.

Cassidy's teasing grin slowly transformed into a knowing one. "Have you told her yet?"

He knew what she meant, and he dropped his gaze to his feet. "I'm not sure if she'll believe me."

"Well, I suppose speaking from experience, if you don't tell her, she'll never know."

twenty-five

The interview room was colder than she'd expected, and Ginny rubbed her arms and tapped her feet while she waited to be called in. The weekend had turned into one giant headache, and she'd spent most of it on a library couch while Lauren worked. Ginny had been too cowardly to stay at home, what with Steven a rock's throw away. He'd attempted to call and text, but she'd given him very straightforward answers or ignored him altogether.

She'd really put herself out there on Thanksgiving. Kissing him was the easiest thing in the world in the moment, but she'd spent all weekend worrying if she'd just had so many firsts with a guy who wasn't ready to be in a relationship. She didn't blame him at all, but it was too embarrassing to face him just yet.

She did remember his eyes, though, when they were in that room. Never once did they leave hers, and they never lingered on her skin when he was helping her get dressed. It didn't feel like he was indifferent to her, but more like he knew just how scary it was for her, and as always, he was her comforting teddy bear.

Her feet shuffled, her heels catching on the chair, and she scolded herself for being so fidgety. She knew enough about interviews to know that half of it was conducted before she even entered the room. So put her hands on her lap and begged her legs to sit still.

The clock ticked away on the wall above a painted landscape picture, each second clacking louder and louder the longer she sat there. Her fingers curled into her skirt, her nails scratching her black nylons. She'd rehearsed the typical interview answers in the mirror, even done a couple of rounds with Lauren, who was a little too eager to do some research on good interview skills. She was ready, she hoped, but she could use a boost.

She pulled her phone out, slamming her eyes shut for a moment. She couldn't expect him to respond, especially since she'd been so good at ignoring him, but maybe just the act of reaching out would calm her nerves.

She woke her screen, and sitting there in her unread messages was a text from Steven.

Good luck today. We're all rooting for you.

Attached was a picture of him and his two puppies. Her heart melted at his sparkling blue eyes, and her feet instantly stilled.

You remembered? she typed back.

His reply was instant. *I remember everything, Gin.*

Her fingers shook over her keypad. What did he mean by that? She wanted to believe he remembered all they shared together and held it precious, like she did. The words wrapped around her like a blanket, and she slid her phone into her purse, content to wait.

The office door opened a few minutes later, and in walked Alex in an out-of-character button-down and slacks. He gave her a head nod and took the empty seat next to her.

"You got the guts to apply, huh, Rummy?" He rested his elbows on his knees, his hands running back and forth against each other. His words were playful, but his tone was off, and a drop of guilt fell into her stomach. Was he still angry with her?

"Mmmhmm," she said. "You, too?"

He shrugged. "Why the hell not, right? Could use the extra bucks."

She bit the inside of her lip. Her heart ran a marathon while her brain tried to find the words. She wanted to get them out before the interviews started.

"Um... Alex?"

"Yeah?"

"I'm sorry about... You know... last week. I didn't mean to offend you or... the girl you were with."

He jerked back, his brow furrowed deep. "What are you talkin' about?"

"Um... Last week? When I sorta... made fun of your night with... a special girl?"

A light came on behind his eyes, and he let out a laugh. "Geez, Rummy. I hadn't given it a second thought."

"Really?"

"A bit more on my mind to be honest." He knocked his shoulder into hers, and a wave of relief fell over her. "But thanks for the apology. Don't sweat it, all right?"

"Okay."

"I kinda liked Teasing Ginny. Make her come out more often."

"I'll... I'll try." She dug up some courage and quipped,

"But once I get this promotion, I won't be seeing much more of you anyway."

He smirked. "Atta girl."

"Ginny Thompkins?" the HR rep asked, stepping into the room. Ginny grabbed the strap of her purse and swung it over her shoulder.

"That's me."

The HR rep gave her a friendly smile and waved her arm out. "We'll be just down this hall."

Ginny followed her lead, patting the pocket in her purse where her phone rested. It was almost as if Steven were there with her, and she held onto that thought as she stepped into the interview room and took control of her future.

***

Ginny fell back onto her bed, sighing at the ceiling with a smile on her face. She'd done it; she'd interviewed with flying colors, only stuttering once during one answer, and eagerly awaited her phone to ring with a resounding yes. She was up against Alex, but she wasn't going to let it bother her. She'd done her best, and she knew dang well that it was good enough.

She lifted the hem of her shirt and gently brushed over the tattoo on her hip. It was slowly healing, getting clearer and less red every day. Every time she saw it she could hardly believe she'd actually gotten a tattoo. It was easily the bravest thing she'd ever done, alongside kissing Steven.

Her thoughts drifted to his hands on her body, his piercing eyes skating over her skin. It wasn't just that he was so handsome or that his kisses were completely addictive. She'd come alive after meeting him, doing things she'd always wanted but was too afraid to do. It was as if he'd clicked a part into place inside of her, connecting the missing link that she couldn't seem to forge herself.

Cocoa's collar jangled as she hopped up onto the bed and nuzzled into Ginny's side. Ginny turned over, curling up with the pup. She wouldn't have Cocoa without Steven, that was for sure. Even if she happened to go to the shelter one day, she never would've asked her landlord to bend the rules for her.

"Hey, girl," she whispered, pressing a kiss to the top of the fluffy dog's head. "I'm so glad we found each other."

Cocoa rolled over, exposing her belly for some scratching. Ginny giggled and obliged, tickling the pup's underarms.

"You know," she mused, "I could say the same thing to Steven..." And she could. It'd be one hundred percent true. She was so grateful they'd met, and there was no way to thank him without telling him exactly how she felt. She wasn't sure he'd reciprocate, or if he was ready to feel anything deep for anyone other than Cassidy, but using her newfound bravery, she decided to tell him anyway.

"He should know," she said out loud, needing to hear it. An idea flickered on in her head, and she playfully scratched Cocoa one more time before rolling off the bed. No matter how fake the relationship might've been for Steven, it was very real for her, and she knew exactly how to say so.

twenty-six

Steven laced up his shoes, ready for another run to clear his head. It'd been a long day, and with only the one response from Ginny earlier, he'd been checking his phone like a madman every few minutes, hoping to hear from her.

He had to get out for a second, let the road take away all of his thoughts. This couldn't be happening again. He couldn't let the girl he loved walk away from him without knowing just how much she meant to him. It was never easy for him to talk about his feelings, but Ginny made things just so… easy. As soon as he could see her face-to-face, he'd let the cat out of the bag. Texting or calling wasn't going to cut it, though he was getting desperate. He'd already texted the words out a million times already before deleting them.

Batman and Robin bounced around at his feet, and he batted them away so he could get the darn shoes tied. "Give me a second, guys," he scolded, and of course they didn't listen. A long, wet tongue flopped from Robin's mouth and licked up the side of his face.

"Ugh," Steven groaned, lifting his shoulder and wiping the drool off with his shirt. The doorbell rang, and the dogs shot toward the front, barking their little heads off.

"Will you stop it?" He pushed the pups from the door with his foot. He peered through the peephole, and his heart leapt from his throat when he saw the top of Ginny's head.

"Okay, guys, privacy time." He hooked their collars with his fingers. "Don't go anywhere, Gin!" he called through the door. "I'm just putting the demon dogs in my room."

He rushed the puppies back there, quickly shutting the door before they could escape. He jogged to the front again, took a deep breath, then swung the door open.

"Hey," he said, a nervous smile pulling his lips. Damn it, she was gorgeous, her hair in a messy side braid that hung over her shoulder and down her chest. Her eyes were wide and shy, like always, and she wore a loose blouse over a short skirt, with black tights covering her legs and sinking into a pair of heeled boots.

"Hey," she said timidly. Her hands were tucked behind her back. "Can I...?" She paused, biting her lip. Steven wanted so much to reach out and hold her, take away that nervous energy passing over them, but he stood stock still.

She closed her eyes and blew out a shaky breath. When she opened them, determination rested in her honey irises.

"Can I borrow some milk?" she asked, holding out a measuring cup. Steven's brow tilted, and he let out a hollow laugh.

"You serious?"

Her shoulders slumped, and she circled her finger around the rim of the cup. "I was... Well, you said you liked our story. You know, about the milk?"

"Uh huh..." His lip curled up, and he leaned against the doorframe, amused by her sweet explanation.

"Well, I thought... So maybe we could still have that story. Without... pretending."

He sighed, tapping the doorknob. "None of it was fake for me, Gin."

"But some of it had to be," she countered. "When would you have fallen out of love with her and fallen into love with—" She sucked her words back into her mouth, a blush running up her neck. He wished he could tell her the exact moment, the exact instant when he fell in love with her, but he couldn't. It was a combination of all of their moments together, and he wasn't sure he could put that into words.

She eyed the cup in her hands. "Look, I do want you to know that I'm just... I'm just so thankful for you. What you've done for me, no one else could've done. You made me come alive, and I've found this new version of me that I really like. And I don't know if I could've become this person without you."

He stepped out of the doorway, and she backed up as he joined her on the porch. His head swam with her beautiful words, and he blinked, trying to make sense of them.

"What are you saying, Gin?"

"I'm saying..." Her eyes lifted to his, and his breath left him completely. "I'm saying... that I think I love you."

She so raw and open and honest. She'd said he had a part in that, but it was all her, and she was braver than he'd ever be.

His hands found her face, and he pulled her up against

him where she belonged. A joyful smile wrapped his mouth, and he shook his head, in awe of her.

"You stole my line," he said, and a wrinkle appeared above her forehead.

"What?"

"I love you, too," he said, his voice sure, his heart leaping from his chest and resting in her pocket. He would gladly let it stay there forever. "I can't tell you when or how or why, but everything about you, about us over the past month was completely real for me. What I felt for Cassidy doesn't compare to what I feel now for you."

A buzz ran over his skin as she stepped into him.

"Really?" she asked, her voice hopeful and breathless. He nodded against her forehead and coaxed her in for a kiss.

Her lips were warm and safe and comfortable and heaven, everything he'd ever dreamed and more. It was the same gorgeous Ginny, but different now that they were truly together. This kiss fused their hearts, and Steven reveled in her, grateful for all the heartbreak and stupid decisions he'd made that led her into his arms.

They broke apart with joyful, goofy grins, and they laughed at each other. Steven swiped her hair from her face. "Official then?" he asked. "You'll be my girlfriend."

She playfully tapped her chin, and he loved seeing her so bold and so shy all at once. It was the perfect blend of Ginny, and he could live with that for as long as she'd let him.

"Depends," she said, holding the measuring cup between them. "How about getting me some milk, and we'll talk about it."

He tossed his head back and snatched her arm. He pulled her inside and within minutes, the milk was long forgotten.

Like the book? Leave a review!
Reviews are a great way to say thank you to the author.

HIS DINNER FOR ONE JUST
GOT COMPLICATED...

Now a sneak peek of

under the tree

romance for all seasons #3

SANDRA MARIE

(Excerpt of Under the Tree, Romance for all Seasons #3. All rights reserved. Unedited and subject to change.)

one

Frankie took a deep breath and let it out slowly. The paper beneath her crinkled as she shifted uncomfortably on the exam table. Faint Christmas music hummed overhead and a few years ago she'd be singing along, letting the spirit of Christmas keep her sane, but she lost the spirit a long time ago.

She'd waited for the doctor to come back with her results for what felt like days. She glanced at her watch, confirming the blackhole phenomena where time goes in slow motion and only happened at doctor's offices was absolutely true. It was the only way to explain that she'd been merely waiting for four minutes.

If only she didn't leave her knitting needles and yarn in the car. She'd been too stuck in her head to remember to grab them. Knitting always had a way to take her mind off of things, make her forget about everything else except for the loops of yarn that she turned into stitches.

She tapped her fingers against her knee and glanced at a very detailed poster of the birth canal. Her heart raced as she took in the size of the baby and... she looked away. It's not like she was pregnant. She was just being cautious. She had plenty of time to meet a guy who was more than just a booty call, even though with his grayish blue eyes, adorable smile paired with her dark brown hair they'd make one beautiful baby. Unfortunately, Alex still acted like a child which was not conducive to raising one.

He could barely take care of himself, too busy partying, doing keg stands and refusing to grow up. He was fun; she couldn't deny that. He brought out the fun side in her, a side that died the day her dad did, but there was a time and place, and Alex didn't know how to separate the two. She felt herself falling for him each time they stumbled into bed together, which she swore would not happen again yet she couldn't resist him no matter how hard she tried.

It was that damn smile and those ridiculously panty dropping eyes that had some magical powers. The memory of those gray orbs started to suck her in, and she shook her head to knock them out of her mind. She and Alex were over. After months of sleeping together she finally—while avoiding direct eye contact—ended it. It was for the best really. She wanted a serious relationship, and love along with the lust but he didn't.

She'd always remember what they had with deep fondness, but it was time to stop pretending they would ever be anything more than friends with benefits.

Another glance at her watch told her three more minutes had passed. She looked at the opposite wall and was met with a gigantic periodic table of a menstrual cycle. She was tempted to swipe her phone up and take a picture to send to Rae, her best friend. How else would she believe the poster existed? But then the door opened, and Dr. Jon

Bateman walked in, holding a clipboard.

He greeted her with a warm smile, and his hazel eyes— the color of the scarf she was currently knitting— glowed with an unmistakable happiness. Frankie assumed that probably had to do with his new girlfriend in the billing department. Rae had filled her in on the gossip after she called Jon to see if he could squeeze Frankie in. Who knew Rae's connection to an OB would one day benefit Frankie?

"So, Francine—"

"It's Frankie."

"Sorry, I'll make a note of that, so I don't forget for next time."

"Next time?" Frankie asked, a lead ball dropping in her stomach. She hoped this would be a one-time deal. He'd tell her she wasn't pregnant, she'd thank him for squeezing her in, and she'd be out of there. "Does that mean…?" She couldn't bring herself to finish the sentence. Not when she was a single woman, still trying to work her way up the ladder at work, had barely any money in savings, and still had to call her mom to ask how to cook chicken.

"You're pregnant," he said, a huge smile settling on his attractive face. His smile should have been uplifting, so why did she feel like she was going to be sick?

She didn't deserve a… She swallowed hard, and the scary word stayed in her throat like a big hot lump. There were so many people who wanted to be… Who were better suited than her. What in the heck was the universe thinking?

Her lips parted, and she wanted to speak, but that dang lump still took up residence in her windpipe. She tried to force words around it, but nothing came out except for a few stuttered sounds.

"Are you sure?" she finally managed. "I mean, how accurate are we talking here?"

"A hundred percent positive. You're going to be a mom."

Fear and panic slammed into her, and a strangled laugh rumbled up her throat and burst out with gusto. Once she started, she couldn't stop, and Dr. Bateman cocked an eyebrow.

"I'm assuming this is a bit of a shock?" he asked.

She managed a nod.

"Do you want me to call someone? The father maybe?"

This time her laugh resembled a bark and ugly emotion mixed together, causing her to hiccup. Sure, doc, go ahead and give Alex a call and tell him his boys can swim like salmon upstream.

"Breathe," Dr. Bateman said. He took a deep breath to demonstrate, and she followed his lead, letting the air fill her lungs then slowly exhaling. Why did she feel like he was using Lamaze moves on her? "I'm going to tell you something I don't tell all my patients."

She pressed her hand to her mouth, and looked at him with curious eyes.

"You're going to be just fine," he said.

A laugh tried to bubble up and over, but she forced it down. "That's your big secret? Wow. I think you need to work on that because it's not all that reassuring."

"You are definitely Rae's friend," he said with a

chuckle. "I don't tell all my patients that because it'd be a lie, and I don't like to lie. Some people aren't ready to be pregnant or have a baby. I can usually tell two minutes after meeting them, but you? I knew right away that you'll be okay."

"How do you know that?" she asked.

"You asked all the right questions. You came here the minute you felt something was off. You listened to your intuition instead of ignoring it like most people do. You're already steps ahead of most."

She looked down at her hands. "I don't feel like I am."

"You are." His insistence was reassuring.

"Just have to have a little more faith in yourself."

He gave her a pat on the shoulder then went back to his clipboard. "I'd say you're about five weeks. A little early for a sonogram, so why don't we schedule one for after the holidays?"

Sonogram. The more he talked the more she couldn't deny or ignore it. She was p…pregnant.

The word bounced around her head while Dr. Bateman continued to speak. The word stayed with her as she made another appointment with the receptionist and even stuck with her as she walked through the cold day and got into her car.

She had a little less than eight months to get used to it.

She grabbed her phone, ripped off her glove, and dialed Rae, tapping her foot patiently against the brake as she waited for Rae to answer. Finally, after an eternity of waiting, Rae's voice boomed through the phone.

"So, are you knocked up or just crazy?"

Frankie went to speak, but once again the words stuck in her throat. A sad noise sputtered out, and she choked back panicked tears.

"Oh my god… you're not crazy."

"Nope," Frankie forced out. "Just pregnant."

"What are you going to do?" Rae asked, her tone lacking its usual zing.

"I'm going to have a baby."

"Alex is going to crap bricks."

"I don't think I'm going to tell Alex," she said. She'd made the decision somewhere between Dr. Bateman telling her she was pregnant and walking out of the exam room. It was for the best. Alex wasn't dad material, and Frankie didn't want him popping in and out of their kid's life like he popped in and out of hers.

She just found out she was pregnant, yet the protective mama bear was already coming out. She didn't want her baby to know loss, and she would do anything to make sure she— or he— didn't.

"Franks," Rae said, "you can't not tell him."

"It's not like he wants to be a dad."

"You don't know that."

"He couldn't even commit to a relationship. What makes you think he can commit to eighteen years of taking care of someone other than himself?"

"You still have to tell him."

"No, I don't."

"You know I'm right. It's not fair to keep this from

him."

There were a lot of things that weren't fair. The fact that it was her who was pregnant and not someone who was married and desperately trying to start a family. The fact that her boss took credit for all the work she recently put into a project. The fact that her favorite restaurant took her favorite entrée off the menu. Or the fact that she couldn't find a guy who wanted to spend time with her outside of the bedroom.

But darn it, she supposed Rae was right. She needed to tell him.

"That silence is you agreeing with me," Rae said smartly. "When are you going to tell him?"

Frankie loved how Rae could read her mind, saving her from speaking about things she'd prefer not to. "I guess now is a better time than any."

"To be a fly on that wall. Call me if he has a heart attack. I'll have to clear my schedule for his funeral."

Frankie laughed, pure and genuine, something she desperately needed. "I will," she said and hung up. She stared at her phone, debating if she should just send Alex a text.

Hey. Guess what? I'm pregnant. Okay bye.

No, that wouldn't be right. This was something she couldn't do through a text or a phone call.

She rested her hand on her stomach, almost instinctively. She wouldn't fall under Alex's spell because this time it wasn't just about her.

It was about her baby.

also by Sandra

Romance for all Seasons

After the Night
Across the Street
Under the Tree
Going Down
Between Friends
Behind the Stick

Summer Nights

Bay Breeze
Tequila Sunrise
Blue Lagoon
Sex on the Beach

about Sandra

Sandra Marie is in love with all things holidays and all things romance! After settling in with a big cup of hot cocoa—with *lots* of whipped cream—she spends her time with quirky and fun characters.

Romance for all Seasons is her debut series

Made in the USA
Columbia, SC
28 May 2022